Accidental Dick
A Billie Ridley Mystery

KAREN BERGER

Cover design by Jennifer Quintenz
Cover photo by Jacob Bercovici

Library of Congress Control Number: 2014919682

ISBN-10: 0692333444
ISBN-13: 978-0692333440

CONTENTS

1

I AM NOT CRAZY

I stood in the bushes peering in the window of my husband's Beverly Hills office, my identity and humiliation hidden beneath a wig and sunglasses. Gary injected fillers into the nasolabial folds of his celebrity patient. He did not kiss or fondle her. I was a fool for doubting him. It started to rain. As his patient left, he stroked her plump cheek. They had a moment. Maybe I was not a fool. A worm that was unearthed in the rain slithered into my shoe. A silent scream and I limped away.

That's how I became a dick.

My age was a secret in those Rodeo Drive days. In the right light I could fake fifties. Long after my periods ceased, I displayed tampons in my bathroom to imply younger. Before Gary, I had been a half-assed actress. Sitcoms, commercials, an improv group, a backup singer. I got fan letters from prison, they made me feel famous.

I was born Billie Ridley. My father named me after Billie Holiday. My mother named me after Billie Burke, the Good Witch in *The Wizard of Oz*. My parents were as unalike as their Billies. Then I married Gary and I became Billie Sontag, Beverly Hills housewife. No fan letters, but better shoes. I had been his patient. He knocked me up and did the right thing. It was the right thing—

we were happy for more years than we weren't. Then I got too old for him, even though we're the same age. It's the cultural hell older women live in. Men can dip thirty years younger. All we wives can dip into is ice cream. In bed in tearstained pajamas, pregnant with Rocky Road.

When Gary came home I was on my second pint. I couldn't confront him. I was the lunatic woman in a wig, hiding in the bushes with a worm in her Ferragamo. Anyway, I wasn't sure. It's not like he fucked her. A look can mean so much more. He smiled at me, and I decided I was a fool. This man loves me. He went to the john with the door open and peed for an eternity.

"It's the diuretics." Familiarity breeds too much information.

He was shooting an infomercial in a few days and pissing himself camera-ready. He, *we*, had a skincare line we were launching. That's another reason I needed to stay married. I wasn't about to give up my half of the company. I showered away my doubts and started making dinner.

Gary got on the treadmill, a nightly ritual to get fit for the infomercial, or so he claimed. When I walked in to announce his mustard-crusted salmon was ready, he was on a sharp incline, drenched in sweat. This was not to pitch a face cream on camera, this was to get naked with some gold digger half his age.

"Why are you doing this?" The treadmill was loud enough for him to pretend he didn't hear me. "Your audience won't believe thin and tan and blindingly white teeth." He ignored me. "I don't trust you or your teeth." Again he ignored me, so I unplugged him.

"What the hell are you doing?!"

"Trying to save us." My poignant delivery trumped his irritation.

He mopped his golden brow. "I know I'm a cliche." A blinding smile. "After the infomercial, I will revert to the pale, potbellied spouse you can believe in." It's amazing how little it takes to win me. I forgave his narcissism, and he forgave my insecurity. We were okay, all was well. Then the phone rang.

Gary leapt to answer it, never a good sign. Some doctorly mumblings, then he walked out with phone in hand. This meant it was a patient, and he would take the call in his study, in case he had to make notes. Or have phone sex with his mistress, as his wife imagined. This scene played out nearly every night. He would go to his study, I'd stand outside the closed door. If the call went on too long, I'd press my ear to a glass and hold it against the wall. It didn't sound like phone sex, unless they were into laser resurfacing. I'd hear him hang up and run to the kitchen. He'd come in and praise my mediocre cooking, and the marriage would resume.

Our one and only child, Emma, came over on her way home from work. "Hello, I must be going" was her standard greeting. Smart, spoiled, she got the best and the worst of both of us. She was on the verge of thirty, but like her mother, she lied about her age. And like her father she lied about her heart. I would lay down my life for my kid. So why didn't I give her more attention when she was little and needed me most? Like all inadequate parents, I was still recovering from my own childhood decades after it ended. Nothing remarkable, I had a needy mother and an absent father who were recovering from their childhoods. Neurotic begets neurotic, and so it goes.

After much floundering in search of a career, Emma landed at a production company that makes reality TV shows. To her credit, she hated her job. "I hear an endless stream of *Hoarders and Tiaras* pitches. All of which I have to take to my boss. There is no telling which abomination the cables will buy."

Fascinating as it wasn't, I listened attentively, compensating for prior neglect. Gary laughed and sympathized in all the right places. She was daddy's little girl, and I loved her so much I wasn't even jealous.

Her visits were a flurry of venting and trying not to eat. She was detoxing and strictly liquid this week. But she surrendered to the salmon, stuffing her mouth as she told Gary to go easy on the self-tanner, he was looking a little orange. Emma departed as abruptly as she had come. Gary and I were adrift again, our glue had gone.

I lay in our bed, waiting for Gary to complete his ablutions—he cleanses and exfoliates. Derms are as rigorous as gays, patients are always checking out their skin. He applied the smelly stuff to darken his hair, then the self-tanner. Still I longed for his slippery

3

orange touch. I made a subtle overture as he got into bed. Then I boldly stroked him, in case I wasn't clear. His rejections were always affectionate and swift.

"I love you to death, but me and my sword are whipped."

"We haven't had sex in eighty-three days." I blurted out my pathetic secret. I had actually been counting. Something in my confession moved him, but not below the waist. He took me in his arms and kissed me with more charity than lust. Any move in my direction felt good. I stayed in his arms until he was asleep, then I crept to the bathroom and began my mandatory, wildly unattractive routine. Gary called it my contribution to the cause. The cause being Sontag Skincare and me being the Guinea Pig in Chief.

Looking in the mirror, I took an inventory of my wrinkles. I applied our anti-aging cream to the *right* half of my face. This was a bit of a cheat, since the right side of every driver's face was less lined. The sun comes in the car window and ages the left side more rapidly. I had been dutifully applying whatever product we were concocting to the right side of my face for years. The good news was, the stuff worked. We would be rich. The bad news was the left side of my face looked like shit.

I had helped with the formula, insisting on squalene to counteract the lactic acid. I was not just the wife, I was half the brains behind the product. It was mine as much as his. He was not going to dump me for some long pair of legs and steal my company!

I do that all the time. It's called a "Jack Story." It's based on an old joke—A traveling salesman gets stuck on a lonely road with a flat tire and no jack. He walks to a service station, talking to himself. "How much can the guy charge me for renting a jack, ten bucks, maybe twenty? It's the middle of the night, if I wake him up he'll want fifty. He'll figure I have no place else to go for a jack and the son of a bitch will want a hundred." Finally, he gets there and yells at the attendant, "Stick your jack up your ass!"

My whole life has been a Jack Story, I always imagine the worst. The problem is, most of the "attendants" I have known have hurt or abandoned me. I decided to cut Gary some slack, it's been thirty

4

years and he's still here.

I stuck a piece of Scotch tape on the vertical eleven lines between my brows to keep myself from frowning. Then I returned to bed. It was crucial that I slept on my back or the cream on the right side of my face would slide to the left. This was not my natural sleeping position. That would be fetal. I put a wedge under my legs so that I didn't roll over. I'd think of Gary waking up to pee and seeing his beloved wedged on her back, her partially wrinkled face, tape between her troubled brows, sagging tits splayed to either side. No wonder he wouldn't do me.

The next day I went to his office. The pretty receptionist greeted me. "I'll let him know you're here, Mrs. Sontag." The entire waiting room looked up from their magazines to see the doctor's wife. I could feel their opinion of Gary diminish. He was a master of the syringe, why did I look so old? At least on the left side.

His pretty nurse summoned me. "Come on back, Billie." Gary's attractive staff was suspiciously nice, smiling as I walked down the hall. Which one was he sleeping with? Was it the blonde in billing? I bet the bitch can't even add. A woman was paying for her treatment and stocking up on Sontag Skincare. He had been peddling it to his patients. It was selling very well. We were ready to go wide. Gary and I put our savings on the line and borrowed the rest. Let him sleep with the whole office—I was about to be more than the wife. I'd be his partner in a multimillion-dollar company, and those you don't dump. A Jack Story with a Joan Crawford ending.

I walked into the examining room and found him injecting Botox into my best friend's neck. Margo is a ballsy Brit with a hacking laugh you can hear from ten tables away at the Ivy. As a publicist, she lunches for a living.

She threw her arm over her head. "Gary's going to paralyze my stinky pits." Her frequent vulgarity is mitigated by a classy English accent. As Gary prepped her armpit, Margo spun her PR plan for our company. She would book him on *The Doctors* just as the infomercial was hitting the air, and she'd ask Uma to rave about it in *Elle*.

As Gary injected the Botox, she commented on his bronze skin and white teeth—"Awfully Erik Estrada for a Jew." Margo uses celebrities as adjectives, a habit of hers I adore and try to emulate.

When Margo departed, Gary stuck the residual Botox in his forehead. He announced he was taking the afternoon off, he had to go to the cosmetic lab that was manufacturing our product. *No, no, I didn't need to come.* Fat chance I wasn't.

We drove to Burbank in our separate BMWs. His was bigger and newer, but I got there first. I competed with him in meaningless ways. The big triumphs were his, the prestige and reputation, but today I beat his ass getting somewhere he didn't want me.

When Gary arrived he seemed worried and worn. He was tired of working so hard. "I've popped enough pimples" was a common refrain. This was his chance to phase out the practice while he still had the cache to launch his own line. I loved him most when he was down, when I feared losing him. Not to another woman, but to death. My father died when I was a kid. Loss has taught me to expect more loss.

The cosmetic lab was a private-label manufacturer. Meaning the formula was ours. We paid them to mass-produce it and do the packaging. Coming here made the dream real. And very expensive. We had been giving them small orders to test on Gary's patients. Now we had the infomercial and meetings with buyers from Nordstrom and Sephora. This was the big time and we had to be ready to deliver. We ordered nine thousand units of each item— cleanser, moisturizer and anti-aging cream. Gary was hardly a pioneer in selling his own product, in fact he was a late bloomer. Murad and Perricone are slathered on upscale skin from Park Avenue to China, and dozens of derms have followed their lead.

A lab tech walked us through the warehouse. First the mixing machine, a giant metal tank filled with a potion that had evolved on my face. Then the filling machines that spit it into jars. Latina girls in paper smocks boxed them as they came down the conveyer belt. I thanked them in my kitchen Spanish. "Gracias por nostra duros trajobamas." I thought I said, "Thank you for your hard work." Apparently, I said something else. They seemed very amused. I am the gringo version of Charo.

Vera, the cosmetic chemist, was a severe woman in a lab coat and glasses. But she did not condescend. Ever since my squalene suggestion, she took me seriously. She examined the right side of my face.

"Not bad for a woman pushing sixty," I boasted.

Gary became transfixed by the labeling machine. It thrust the jars forward like little soldiers and slapped Gary's name on them. He was quietly overcome. "I'm a brand." I was upset we spent so much on the packaging, the money should go into the ingredients. No container ever made a woman look better.

My cell phone rang, interrupting Gary's reverie. It was my mother, she was in a perpetual state of need so I was willing to ignore her. But Gary said go, he would stay at the lab, watching over his brand. It was *our* goddamn brand.

My mother, June, lives in a Glade-scented apartment in the Wilshire corridor. No one knows her exact age, all evidence of it has been destroyed. A former chorus girl, she still wears pancake makeup, eyeliner, and rouge. She puts on her face no matter what—surgeries, earthquakes, she will not be unmasked. Her hair is a Clairol strawberry blond worn in an updo from the '40s. The bangs are hers, but the topknot is augmented by a hairpiece, it sits on her head like a dead cat of curls.

A fairly decent singer and dancer, she was in *Carousel* and *South Pacific*. When my father died, she had to take a job as a secretary, and her musical-comedy life ended. After a long stint as a single mother, she married Ned, the vacuum-cleaner king. All of this was in New York where I was born and raised. My home is here, but I belong there. When Ned retired they moved to Florida. He died, and she descended on Los Angeles and her daughter. She's outlived everyone she ever loved. All she has is me and one last sister in Palm Springs. I find that very moving. If she wasn't so exasperating, I would have more sympathy, but all she inspires is guilt.

June has a long list of maladies, none of them lethal, just enough to keep me on call and hauling her to doctors. Gout, GERD, bronchitis, arthritis, stenosis, thrombosis, all her organs are out of warranty. Her dementia only manifests when it's

7

convenient, so I believe it to be voluntary. I do all her shopping and organize her millions of meds. Keeping her alive is killing me.

It was a typical thankless afternoon with Mom. I filled her refrigerator—"That's the wrong milk," she says. I hung up her dry cleaning—"So many ruffles and no place to go." I called her podiatrist—"What good are feet that forgot how to dance?"

I sat down to do her meds, putting them in plastic sticks with a little compartment for each day of the week. There was a stick for morning and another for evening. It took me a soap opera and a game show to fill them. June stared at the TV as I rambled on about my marriage.

She focused on me briefly. "Spice things up a little, get some fishnet stockings."

As I dispensed her medication, I pondered my mother's sexual history. She had been a chorus girl, not a nun. I pictured her in fishnets and all that rouge. She was beautiful in her prime. I bet she got laid more than me.

I stopped at the mall on the way home to buy some sexy lingerie. Three-way mirrors can be so cruel. The push-up bra created mounds of back fat, the garter belt accentuated my fallen ass, my flabby white thighs poked through the fishnet. As we get older, the meat starts coming off the bone. It hangs there in relentless descent until we die and insects feast on our remains. These were my thoughts as I assessed my rear view. A shapely customer and a salesgirl giggled as they walked by.

"When you're my age, remember this day and see how funny it feels," I said. It turns out they were giggling at a Yorkshire terrier that had escaped from the customer's purse. He attacked my marabou mules in defense of his mistress. I laughed my fallen ass off. We bonded, and the girls gave me some tricks to try in the bedroom. I paid for my purchases and received a 10 percent discount on the chewed mules.

I was lying on the bed in my slutty ensemble. It didn't look bad from the front. I arranged and rearranged myself in various poses. I got bored and tied myself to the headboard with silk ties, using my teeth. Where the hell was Gary? The candles were dripping, my arms were numb. Two hours later, he came home. His reaction did not match my fantasies. He looked at me like I was crazy.

I stuck to my script. "Do whatever you want with me."

"Hold that thought." He fled to the bathroom and peed for an eternity. "It's the diuretics."

He returned to the bedroom, and I continued the seduction. When he couldn't think of anything he wanted to do to me, except get me some professional help, he untied me. After the feeling came back in my arms, I tried the tricks the girls taught me. He regarded me with raised eyebrows, but nothing else rose up. I suggested Viagra, which he declined. I dropped to my fishnet knees to no avail. Then I gave up. Gary fell asleep with a protective hand over his sword.

The next morning we couldn't look at each other. He left for the office, and I sling-shot the elastic garter belt across the bedroom. It landed on a framed photograph of Gary and me when we were young and in love. I cried for a while and then I got mad. He couldn't get it up because he was out of bullets. Not even a mercy hump. I was convinced he was having an affair. I didn't eat, I didn't sleep. I snooped. It was a lot like sex. My heart would race, I'd breathe hard. It was bad, it was wrong, and so exciting.

I went through all his credit card receipts. I'd wait until he fell asleep and take his cell phone to a distant closet, checking every call and text, dialing unidentified numbers. If a woman answered I went wild. I read his e-mail, lurked on Facebook, checked to see what he bought on Amazon. He had an answer for everything, but I knew better.

I planted an earring in his car and then pretended to find it, demanding to know who it belonged to. He claimed he didn't know. *What a liar.* It could have been hers for all he knew. Whoever she turned out to be, I'm sure she wore earrings.

At two in the morning I stole his keys and broke into his office to put a Nanny Cam in an artificial fern. I was almost done when the police came, responding to a silent alarm. I explained it was my husband's office, and I had every right to be there . . . in the middle of the night, in black sweats and a ski hat. When Gary arrived, they asked him if he knew me. He looked at me a long time and said he didn't know me at all anymore.

We went home and fought till dawn. I said he was gaslighting me, making me think I was crazy for suspecting him. He said I was gaslighting myself. There was no other woman in his life except for my paranoid, earring-planting alternate personality. I was destroying the marriage, he begged me to go to a shrink before it was too late.

Dr. Elliot Krasny is a short man, sixty-something, with a slight accent. There is a twinkle in his eyes and wisdom in his words. Right away, he made me feel safe. I told him about my recent antics. He said they didn't matter, except as clues to why. This led to my father—Murray sold insurance and was always on the road. He died in a car accident when I was six. He was driving home in the rain.

"No wonder you fear losing a man." It wasn't only the truth of what he said, but Krasny's caring expression. I wept as I told him about my long lost father.

"Murray's mother was Irish. His father was Jewish—some immigration officer at Ellis Island changed the name to Ridley. They lived on the Lower East Side, just off Delancey."

Krasny smiled, he knew Delancey, or maybe he knew me and how much I needed his warmth.

"I remember Murray's footsteps on the stairs. He wore a tweed overcoat and brown shoes. He looked at me like he loved me." A long silence. "He was gone too often, and then he was gone for good."

Murray was alive in this room, and I never wanted to leave. When the precious forty-five minutes were up, Krasny saw me to the door. He could see me next Thursday. I told him to drive very carefully until then.

I told Gary all about Krasny, extending my forty-five-minute memory of another man. Gary was a little jealous. But happy for me, happy for us. I said I was sorry for all my crazy shit. We were friends again, all was well. Until we shot the infomercial.

Duffy Direct Marketing was the largest production house on the West Coast. Mrs. Duffy was Gary's patient and "addicted" to his products. She encouraged her powerful husband to take us on. This included the script, hiring all the sincere women to do the testimonials, the media buys, the call center. We mortgaged the house and took the plunge.

Gary was sweating like a stuffed pig in his man spanx and Armani suit. "It's the diuretics," he said to the makeup girl who powdered him down. Duffy and the director insisted Gary wear the traditional doctor's white coat with *Dr. Sontag* embroidered on the breast. All those miles on the treadmill for naught. Gary agreed to wear the coat.

He went to the set and stood under the lights. Sweat poured down his face. They brought in a wind machine and trained it on Gary. His artificially dark hair blew back in the wind, not a credible look for a doctor. They solved this with another fan that blew in the opposite direction. His hair was at rest. They tried to do a take. The only line he got right was his name.

Nineteen takes later, Dr. Sontag found his place in the spotlight. Harriet Bloom, the spokeswoman hired to host, asked him about the products. He responded with lawyer-approved copy and added some handles as he grew into his role.

"Well, Harriet," a blinding smile, "the lactic acid opens the pores, allowing the retinol to penetrate deeper into the dermis." Duffy was worried it sounded too dirty. They changed "penetrate" and kept the smile.

I was stuck in a corner with friends and family. Emma, who knew from TV production, would walk on the set periodically to advise her father. Our team from the lab came by, Vera and the packaging guy. Margo had to leave, an actor went skinny dipping in the Beverly Hilton pool, and she had to do damage control.

I'd had enough of the corner. I walked over to Duffy and struck up a conversation. He was bored before I opened my mouth. I told him how we developed the product on half my face, the ingredients were the result of my trial and error. He cut me off and told me never to tell that story again. It detracts from the acclaimed dermatologist if the wife takes any credit. And so I faded back into the corner.

The last thing they shot was a model, Tawny, rubbing the moisturizer into her flawless face. After each take, she'd wipe it off and start over again. Gary grew more enamored with every application. Tawny smiled at his one-liners about how moist she was getting.

Mrs. Duffy attempted to comfort me. "The models always upset the wives."

But it was Vera, the cold-fish chemist, who needed comforting. Behind her glasses, she was glaring at Gary as if she'd been horribly wronged. She welled up, barely beating her tears out the door. I was not having some paranoid fantasy, this was real.

The day after we shot the infomercial, Gary called me from his office and said he had to go to the lab, there was a problem with the emulsifier in the cleanser.

A good lie is all in the details. I told Gary I was taking June to Encino for her periodontist's memorial and would be home late. June was very upset that Dr. Moreland went "on tour" (my mother's euphemism for dead), no one knew her gums like he did.

I got to the lab after six. Gary's car was in the parking lot. I drove down the block and left my car where it wouldn't be seen. I was back in the wig and sunglasses, spying on my husband. I went to the side of the building and stood on a plastic crate, peering through the ventilation window of Vera's lab. My eyes narrowed as I looked through the metal slats. Vera had to be forty, but she looked good without the lab coat and glasses.

They kissed and I stopped breathing.

Gary pulled away. "I can't do this anymore." Vera railed as he explained why he couldn't divorce me. "Billie would get half of everything." There it was, the awful truth.

"I'm sick of hearing about your idiot wife!"

"She's getting suspicious. And I'm feeling guilty."

Vera threw a beaker of argon oil at Gary. "You used me!" Then she threw her arms around him and sobbed. He tenderly peeled her off.

"I can't leave Billie." He paused and said softly, "I still love her." His idiot wife could breathe again.

I ran to my car and followed him home over Laurel Canyon. I was devastated, but at least he broke it off. My feelings went back and forth with every curve—I love him, I hate him. I'll take him back, right after I kill him. We got to the bottom of the canyon and

Gary made a left turn onto Sunset. Home was in the opposite direction.

My cell phone rang. It was Gary. "Hi, honey, it's me, I'm still stuck at the lab." I stopped breathing again. "How's it going with June?"

"I'm still in Encino," I lied. We said our good-byes and then Gary pulled into an all-night diner. Clearly he didn't want to be seen by anyone he knew. I parked down the street, slapped on my wig and walked back to the diner.

The model, Tawny, pulled into the parking lot. I stood outside the diner for an hour. They finally came out, got in his car and drove off together. I couldn't make up a Jack Story this bad. I cried my way home and plotted my revenge.

The next day, I had lunch with Margo. She got drunk. I ordered every carb on the menu and told her about my sleuthing, wigged out and peering in windows. "Gary won't give me half the company without a fight. He can't know that I know until I have proof. Dr. Sontag's infomercial fans won't like him fucking the model and dumping his wife!"

"That bastard will never inject me again." Margo took my shattered marriage so badly it made me inquire about her own marriage. She threw back more wine. "That's a whole other lunch, my darling."

I went home to Gary and masked my fury. I spit on his omelet and served it with a smile. I put green dye in his self-tanner and admired his chartreuse tan. I sprinkled cayenne pepper in his designer briefs and waved him off scratching his crotch. He never suspected his dutiful wife was his assailant. When he was at work, I watched home movies of our marital history. Vacations, anniversaries, Emma's graduation, Gary and me dancing a tango. Was he cheating on me then? Probably. I just didn't want to know it.

I cancelled my appointment with Dr. Krasny—I didn't want wisdom to cloud my thinking. I told Gary an elaborate lie about taking June to see her ailing sister in Palm Springs. I put the video camera in a duffle bag, along with the power drill I got Gary for Christmas. I tossed in my wig, black sweats, and a box of chocolate truffles for the road. I walked out the door of my unhappy home and went to war.

I rented a nondescript Ford to tail Gary. Wearing the wig and licking chocolate from my fingers, I followed him to a motel in Malibu. It was October and the beach was deserted. Gary went to his room, and then Tawny arrived. I paid double to get the room next to theirs. They went out to dinner, and I drilled a hole in my closet wall. I set up the video camera and looked through the hole into Gary's room, adjusting the lens to get a better view of the bed.

When they came back from dinner, I turned on the camera. Gary got in bed as the Viagra kicked in. He professed his profound titillation, and Tawny responded by removing her bra. I let the camera be my witness and went out the sliding glass door. I crawled over my balcony onto theirs and walked into their room. Tawny screamed and Gary clutched his chest. I sat on the bed and faced the camera, making sure I was in the frame. They were too distracted to notice the hole in the wall.

I complimented Tawny on her firm flesh. "Gary's a derm, he's into skin, you make the perfect couple. His skin is looser but his wallet is thicker, so it's a fair trade. The one so many trophies make. In ten years he's in dentures, and you get fat and fuck the pool man." I smiled at Gary and summed up my thesis. "The idiot wife gets half your wallet and lives happily ever after. Vera had it all wrong—you're the idiot husband."

Gary freaked out. "Did Vera call you?"

I continued to astonish him. "Telling your middle-aged mistress you couldn't leave me, then off to the diner and the younger model."

"How could you possibly know that?"

"I know everything." I took a lucky guess. "I even know about Claudia." Claudia was the blonde in billing.

"How long have you known about her?"

"I think I've always known." I realized how long I had been lying to myself. "Asshole." I meant me, but Gary assumed I meant him.

He said I didn't understand him. Accusations flew back and forth, right over Tawny's head. I challenged his manhood. "You never even touch me!"

"I can't fuck a sixty-seven-year-old woman!" My real age, revealed at the top of my husband's lungs.

Tawny tried to reassure me. "You don't look a day over fifty."

"At least not on the right side," Gary added.

I seized the opportunity to make my case. "I spent years testing formulas on half of my face so we could build a company and this is the thanks I get." Then I detailed my contribution to the cause.

Gary mimicked my loud and clear annunciation. "Thank you very much."

I turned toward the camera. "Did you hear that, judge?"

Gary spotted the hole in the wall and went over to investigate, giving himself an inadvertent close-up. He looked in the hole and saw the camera. "Oh, my God."

I walked out of that motel room with half our company and a broken heart. The married chapter of my life was over.

2

DOWNTOWN GIRL

I told Emma to meet me at my mother's. I had to do June's meds and might as well tell them the bad news together. Emma walked in and said, "Hello, I must be going." She had to get back to work, one of their reality stars had liposuction and died on the table.

I got right to the point. "Gary and I are getting a divorce."

"Whatever he's done, you must forgive him," my mother said.

I told her I couldn't, there had been other women. Emma didn't flinch, I realized she already knew. I guess everyone did.

"You should just keep the man and the life," my mother insisted.

"What makes you so sure? Did Ned cheat on you, or God forbid, my father?" June had a bout of convenient dementia so I didn't pursue it.

"I'm sixty-seven years old. This is my third act and I want a good ending." I had uttered my age aloud. My mother and daughter concealed their ages. By outing myself, I outed them. The intergenerational deception had to end. I told them I planned to embrace my age and sang my version of the Beatles lament—"*Will you still need me, will you still fuck me, when I'm sixty-seven?*" June was having palpitations, so I returned to the safer subject of my divorce. "I'm getting half the business, but we're fighting over the house. Thirty years and all that matters to him is the money."

Emma burst into tears. I tried to reassure her. "Both of us will always love you."

But that wasn't her problem. Emma confessed she was sleeping with her married boss. "He'll never leave his wife, it costs too much money."

My little girl was the other woman. What was a mother supposed to say? Her demented grandmother knew what to say— "Maybe his wife will get liposuction and die."

Each of us took one of June's Valiums and called it a night.

Gary refused to move out of the house, so I kept the bedroom and he slept in the guest room. The kitchen was a communal room where we did most of our fighting. The phone rang. I got there first. The female voice claimed to be Gary's patient.

"Does he inject you with fillers or poke you with his sword?" I asked. Gary went ballistic and I hung up. The phone rang again. An actress was due on the set in the morning, and her face was a catastrophe. Gary grabbed the phone and ran to his study, locking the door. The phone rang all night. Several patients were in distress.

The waiting room in Gary's office was filled with itchy red faces. Claudia, the whore in billing, was one of the swollen. Gary blamed allergies, psoriasis, their home microdermabrasion kits. But the only thing they had in common was his anti-aging cream. Dr. Sontag and his estranged wife were in panic mode.

Gary called the lab. Their lawyer called us back—it was Gary's formula, they were not responsible, as their contract clearly states. We called the suppliers of suspicious ingredients, they had no other incidents with their retinol or lactic acid. The accusations were circular, legal action was threatened all-around. Gary's brand was a lawsuit in a jar.

Mrs. Duffy arrived at Gary's office with an irritated face and decollete. Mr. Duffy pulled the infomercial with its money-back guarantee before it ever aired. The stores we courted cancelled their orders and Sontag Skincare was off the shelf. Gary's high-profile patients abandoned him, he was dead in Hollywood, his waiting room relegated to acne and ingrown hairs. Tawny was dating a plastic surgeon.

Gary went down in flames and I went with him. The kitchen table was stacked with insurmountable bills. Our lawyer, Mickey Stinger, was Gary's college roommate, a loud-mouth DeVito who had the hots for me way back when. Most of our money went to Mickey. He even handled the divorce—there was nothing to fight over, split the debts down the middle and sell the house before the bank does. Friends and neighbors fell away, the nouveau poor of Beverly Hills were as welcome as herpes.

We put the house on the market. Only the desperate sell in October, and so we kept lowering the price. Gary and I stayed on opposite ends of the house. If we had any encounters, one of us tended to throw something. I'd hide his remote, he'd eat my Mallomars. He'd play jazz and I'd retaliate with the Stones, singing along, right in his face. I'm a passionate rocker and incredibly loud, a cross between Jagger and Merman. Margo called the last days of my marriage *War of the Sontags—A Cautionary Musical*.

One night Gary didn't come home. He could be dating or dead, what was it my business? Still I couldn't sleep. I tried turkey, warm milk, melatonin, masturbation. Five miles on the treadmill. A *Law and Order* marathon.

I spent the rest of the night in the bathroom, restoring the left side of my face. I applied Retin-A, then sealed it into my pores with a moisturizer. Scotch tape on my eleven lines. I put a second piece of tape across the bridge of my nose, waited five minutes and peeled it off, blackhead free. When I could afford it, I'd get all the Botox and fillers my face could hold. Other derms would love to say they treat Gary Sontag's ex. Maybe they'd trade me a vial of Juvederm for the brag.

The house finally sold, and we had to be out in thirty days. We liquidated our lives. I traded the BMW for a used Civic. We sold what we could on Craigslist. Then we had that most embarrassing of events—a Beverly Hills garage sale. One of Gary's face-cream victims showed up and demanded the espresso maker as restitution.

Gary's brother, Ronald, bought a lamp to justify his visit, but he was there to gloat. Like their father, Ronald was a cardiologist.

They never approved of Gary's medical specialty or his wife. Gary would be staying with Ronald until he got on his feet. It seemed a fitting punishment.

Strangers picked through our possessions. Cleo Watson paid two grand for a slightly damaged dining room set. She was big, black, and hard to forget. We sat at the dining table which was on the front lawn, eating Doritos. Gary and I shared a glare. She felt my pain. "I been there, baby, I got a big love for a bad man." We commiserated and hugged good-bye. My dining room set would have a good home.

Margo dropped by with her husband, George, an interior designer. Years ago he sold me a credenza for four thousand dollars. He wrote me a check and bought it back for five. My friends were so much cooler than Gary's. Unmarried doesn't mean unloved.

I cranked up Prince on Emma's old boom box to celebrate my independence. Gary countered with Count Basie. The gardener bought the boom box for a fast twenty. Emma chided me for selling her memories. She suddenly treasured every discarded remnant of her childhood. How could I put a price on her Astronaut Barbie? In a blatant effort to out-parent me, Gary wrapped his arms around Emma. "We'll put your stuff in storage and save it for your daughter."

Hopefully not fathered by her married boss, I said to myself.

My nephew, Stella, arrived and instantly improved my mood. He is a drag queen who does everyone from Gaga to Garland. Today he was "early Madonna" in leather and lace. Stella's real name is Stanley. When he was sixteen he put on a dress and never looked back. It bothered Gary that I was so tight with the black sheep of the family. Stella was the pompous Ronald's only son.

"Daddy dearest." Stella kissed Ronald on both cheeks, branding him with red lipstick.

Ronald withdrew and pulled out his pager. "I have to be in surgery."

"What kind of fool lets you fuck with his heart?" Stella said as his father fled his company. Margo's hacking laugh was to let Ronald know whose side she was on.

I used to trip all over my pronouns when referring to Stella. But he . . . *she* got sick of me correcting myself and told me to call her *him*. Stella was moving to New York, and I was subletting his loft in downtown LA. It was run-down and dirt cheap, which was all I could afford.

Our greedy little lawyer, Mickey, rolled by in his Bentley and collected all the money we made. The credenzas and Barbies barely made a dent in what we owed.

Gary complained he could never retire. "I'll be popping pimples till I'm ninety."

At least he had a marketable skill. I had no idea what I'd do. Actors my age couldn't get arrested. I could always get a job at Macy's. Every financially desperate woman of a certain age says that. Soon we'll all be working at Macy's, and there will be no customers. We'll stand behind our counters selling handbags to each other.

Gary and I spent our last night under the same roof avoiding each other. Then we both found our way to the communal kitchen. He gave me a sad smile. "I'm sorry." The son of a bitch could still move me. Just when I was in danger of missing him, Gary saved me. "I met someone. I think I'm in love." I got in my used Civic and went to the market. Five pints of discounted ice cream got me through the night.

The next morning I picked up two Latino guys outside Home Depot, Jose and Romeo. I amused them with my garbled Spanish as they loaded the U-Haul with boxes. There wasn't much to move, we'd sold everything we owned. I kept the bed and Ralph Lauren linen. From a ten-room house to a run-down loft. The next stop is a tiny room in assisted living with barely a chair to call my own. It turns out there's a lot you can live without.

I climbed in the U-Haul with Jose and Romeo and bid Beverly Hills adios. On the way downtown, I drove past the Troubadour where I once waited tables. Lousy tips, but some great shows. I saw Pryor, Elton, Leon Russell, long before they hit. I continued through West Hollywood, past the hardware store where I met my first husband. Archie was a comic and part-time carpenter. It was the seventies, so he had long hair and a beard. He told this story in his act—"I was walking down the street carrying two pieces of wood, a trucker drives by and says, 'Hey, Jesus, your cross is broken.'" He was funny and he could build a table, so I married him. Then I found out he was a manic-depressive, or so I chose to believe. He was madly in love or sleeping in his car to avoid me. We stayed together four years, half of them were maniacally happy.

I reminisced about past loves as I passed LA landmarks that brought them to mind. There was too much traffic on memory lane, so I got on the freeway. It was bumper-to-bumper by Western. On my right was a Rolls with an older man and a younger woman. The better the car, the bigger the gap. On the other side of me was a Volvo with two older women. Thirty years ago *Newsweek* reported a woman over forty has a better chance of getting killed by a terrorist than getting married. Today the odds are so bad the terrorist would have to be Belgian.

I could see the downtown skyline. It looked like a mini-Manhattan. I got off the freeway and hit the street. It was teeming and multicultural. Homeless guys with shopping carts next to hedge fund guys in limos. The gentrification was erratic—the Staples Center, Skid Row, Disney Concert Hall, Little Tokyo. High-rise hotels towered over fire traps. Stella lived in one of the fire traps. My new hood was industrial and vaguely dangerous.

"Toto, we're not in Beverly Hills anymore." Jose and Romeo laughed at my Spanish as I tried to explain my musing.

The small, dilapidated building was older than me. Three stories of worn brick and a fire escape. It used to be a factory that made men's hats, then it was converted into lofts. The paint was chipping off the walls, the floors were cracked. It reminded me of my grandmother's building on the Lower East Side where my father grew up. I like anything that brings him back. Maybe I'd be okay here.

Stella came out to greet me looking like J.Lo in a big-hair wig and low-cut dress. Romeo was instantly smitten. I explained the gender issue in Spanish. Apparently, I misspoke. Romeo kissed Stella's hand and fist bumped Jose, whatever that meant.

Stella took me upstairs to see my new reality. Nine hundred

square feet of concrete and no insulation. You froze or melted, depending on the season. He opened a window and showed me the fire escape which he called a *terrace*. There was a toilet and shower in a tiny cubicle he called a *bathroom*. The thing he called a *kitchen* was a stove and fridge shoved against a wall. A giant wooden table from the factory days separated the kitchen from the rest of the loft. It served as counter, dining table, and desk. One barstool was the only seating. I wouldn't be doing much entertaining.

Romeo leered as Stella filled a suitcase with sexy dresses and platform pumps. Stella had an amazing closet, and I was welcome to borrow anything that fit. My clothes seemed so dull hanging next to Cher's chaps.

Stella had to leave for the airport, but first he wanted me to meet my neighbors. Hacker lived across the hall—a self-described neo-geek who wore a pocket protector with pens and a joint. His spiked hair and horn-rimmed glasses were set against pale skin that never saw daylight. A former Silicon Valley rogue, he was creating software to protect computers from people like him. Hacker said how much he'd miss Stella's impersonations and could I do Julia Child when he got hungry? He was smart and potentially useful, I'm technologically challenged.

Stella clomped down the stairs in stilettos and introduced me to Ivan the Asshole. The tags to his name were optional. Ivan the Untalented, Ivan the Lecher. He was a painter in his forties with piercing eyes and a booming voice, a flamboyant has-been that never really was. It was Candy, Ivan's muse, that Stella wanted me to meet. Candy's breathy Monroe was so broad that at first I thought she might be in drag. But she was too pretty to be a guy, and the Monroe was sincere. Marilyn was Candy's religion, she can recite her whole life, chapter and verse. Ivan slapped Stella's padded ass as a farewell. Candy hugged Stella, their ample bosoms colliding. Then Candy hugged Aunt Billie and promised to take good care of me.

Stella wanted me to meet the musician who lived below me, but Harpo wasn't home. *Harpo?* I told Stella I was a terrible sleeper. "Bang on the pipes and he'll turn it down." And with that disturbing advice, Stella handed me his keys and headed for New York.

I cleaned and scoured the loft. When I went to take a shower, the water came out in rusty spurts. The toilet was even worse. It didn't flush, it exploded. Didn't Stella ever take a piss? Why didn't he mention the ear-shattering, water-splattering toilet? I looked at myself in the mirror. That was more alarming than the toilet. The bathroom had bad lighting! The horrified woman staring back at me looked her age.

I was too tired for an ice cream run. I'd comfort myself with chicken noodle soup. But I couldn't get the stove to light. The cold soup offered little comfort. I sat on Stella's mildewed couch to watch TV. The picture was snowy so I listened to *The Good Wife*. That's when I noticed the flashing red letters on the wall—B A D A B A N G. What did it mean? I looked out the window. It was coming from the neon sign on the bar across the street. I didn't know whether to laugh or cry, and so I did both. Was this a nervous breakdown? I'd go back to Dr. Krasny as soon as I could afford him.

Suddenly, there was a loud incessant noise. Beep, beep, beep, beep. It was a backup beeper from an 18-wheeler, perfectly synced with the flashing red lights. Drums and a pounding bass came from below. It was Harpo. I started banging on the pipes with one of Stella's spiked heels, it made a hole in the pipe and water gushed out. I plugged the hole with Stella's eyeliner pencil. I was soaking wet. It was so cold I could see my breath.

I crawled into my Beverly Hills bed and wrapped myself in my past. I finally fell asleep and had a terrifying dream—Gary was cheating on me, and then we went broke. We sold the house, and I was living in a loft with bad lighting.

3

A DICK IS BORN

I kept trying to wake up and make it go away, but this was no nightmare, this was my life. The sun was shining in my eyes. I dragged myself out of bed. I needed structure, something familiar. I got out my trusty digital scale. It's remarkably consistent, I can get off and on ten times and get the same reading. I peed first and mounted it naked as I always do. Cold soup and a breakdown was a great diet, I lost two pounds. Jane Fonda said something I love. "Children see their worth reflected back to them in their parents' eyes." That's how I feel about my scale. It looks into my soles and tells me my worth in big black digital numbers.

I looked in the bathroom mirror. The lighting was better. Or maybe I actually looked better, I just needed sleep. Maybe the mirror was as accurate as the scale. Should we believe the good lighting or the bad?

Margo arrived with lox and bagels. I gave her the barstool and took the mildewed couch. Her hacking laugh filled the loft as I told her about my misadventures in my new home. The worst of times make the best of stories. Yesterday's busted pipe is tomorrow's guffaw. Perhaps I could be a stand-up comic and talk about my plumbing. Only the young go to comedy clubs, and they like their jokes dirty. I could open a club for seniors. But they like their jokes too clean. I'm somewhere in between—a hard-core mouth from a

PG generation. How was I going to make a living? I had to pay my rent, plus food, gas, insurance, mascara.

Margo's hacking laugh became a whimper. She told me her husband was having an affair. George is younger than Margo and better looking, but he's a good guy, buying back credenzas from a friend in need. It was Margo who strayed over the years. "On press junkets there's nothing to do but eat or screw. If George knew, he didn't seem to care. Our sex life has become a semiannual event reserved for holidays or reaffirming life after someone dies." George is an A-list interior designer, which fed Margo's theory about her rival. "She's some fucking Aniston who fell for his impeccable taste."

Margo made me a proposition that dramatically altered my future. She wanted me to investigate George's dalliance, like I did with Gary. "Dust off your wig, fire up the drill, whatever it takes." She needed to know how serious it was. And I needed a job. Our problems were a perfect fit. She would pay me with her Hermes Kelly handbag, which sold for seven grand. It was a gift from the studio for keeping an actor's DUI off *TMZ*. She thrust the leather bag in my lap and stroked it. I could take it to lunch or turn it into cash. But George was my friend, I didn't want to bust him. Stroke, stroke. I was bought for the price of a purse.

There was a rhythmic rapping on my door. It was Harpo. He handed me a frying pan. "Use this to bang on the pipes, otherwise you might spring a leak." I told him I was already leaking, but repaired it with Stella's eyeliner pencil. This produced a smile.

Harpo is a downtown hippie in his thirties, with thrift-store clothes and a mop of curls. I asked if he was related to his famous namesake.

"My great aunt was born in Alsace, which is where Harpo's father was from."

"The Marx brothers were French?" Go figure.

Margo said she had to go. She pointedly put the Kelly bag on the counter. Ever the publicist, she was spinning my reputation. "Thank you for taking my case."

Harpo looked at me with more interest. "What do you do?"

Margo answered, "Billie is a private detective."

Word spread around the building and I became known as Billie the Dick. I sold the Kelly bag on EBay and went to work. Margo gave me George's schedule. I looked for holes in his routine, when he might have time for a tryst. I called the Design Center, his dentist, he was always where he was supposed to be.

It was time to take my act into the field. I retired my wig. Stella had a dozen of them in every color and style. I was feeling mysterious and Dietrich, so I went with the ethereal blond. I bought myself a trench coat at Ross. It was fun, like playing a part.

I had Margo tell George she was going out of town on a press junket. I got in my Civic and followed him all over town. He had dinner with a statuesque brunette. I got a table and ordered the cheapest thing on the menu. I only heard snippets of their conversation. She wanted a sink in her island. Was George doing her or her kitchen? They laughed and drank wine. He got a remodeling job, and I paid twenty-two bucks for some stuffed mushrooms. They parted company in the parking lot without so much as a grope.

The wind howled as I followed George to a house in Santa Monica. It was cozy, inviting, the kind of place you park a mistress. He smoothed his hair before using his key to go inside. My video camera was broken, Gary had smashed it during the War of the Sontags. I had to make do with the camera on my iPhone. I waited long enough for something incriminating to happen and climbed the fence into the backyard. There were two towels beside the bubbling hot tub. My heart raced, my hands shook, and it wasn't even *my* husband. I had a perfect view of the bedroom which was lit with candles.

George was in the bed. "Get in here, honey, I'm hard as a rock."

His male lover came bounding out of the bathroom and somersaulted onto the bed, landing in the splits. He was upside down, inside out, contorting his middle-aged body into a series of acrobatic positions. I was spellbound, then I finally remembered to take pictures. A gust of wind blew Stella's wig into the hot tub. I fell in trying to fish it out. I drove home in my steaming trench coat wondering how to tell Margo what I witnessed.

I called her and said we needed to talk. She desperately wanted to know and desperately didn't. I was to meet her at the Polo Lounge for lunch, she liked her bad news with a whiskey chaser. I don't drink, I overeat. I was mainlining the parmesan fries when Margo arrived. Every time I tried to tell her about George, she took a call or worked the room. When I was on my second dessert, I blurted it out.

"You were right, he has a lover." I don't know if it was nerves or the memory of George's bizarre sexual partner, but I started to giggle. "It's a man." I couldn't suppress my laughter. "A very limber man." I showed her the picture on my iPhone and laughed again.

"If you laugh one more time, I shall strike you." And she did. Then we both laughed. And cried. It was so intimate and raw. We had never been closer.

Margo demanded I be there when she confronted George. The obscenities were slung in an icy English accent. "Who is your limber lover, this flexible fuck?" She insisted on calling him "Limber" and that's who he became. "Are you in love with him?"

George admitted he was and went on to explain Limber's agility. "He was an acrobat in *Cirque du Soleil*. He got too old to perform and became a real estate agent. That's how we met, he sold a house that I did. I'd always been sexually uncertain, but when he cartwheeled into my arms, I knew he was the one."

Eventually, George forgave me. Now he could be who he really was. He and Margo parted as friends, they were both too wonderful to lose. She kept the house. George moved in with Limber. So it all worked out, I had earned my purse.

I was the only budding private detective with a promoter. Margo got me another case. "You're a dick women can relate to. You've been in their Louboutin shoes."

She told me about my prospective client. Felicia was a striking Bacall in her mid-thirties. Her adulterous husband was Mike Armstrong, money manager to the stars and cocksman extraordinaire. He grew up in the Bronx, and Felicia gave him class. "I told her you specialized in infidelity. You nailed my husband and countless others, but were so discreet I didn't know their names." I needed the money, but this was too big a bluff.

Margo kept selling. "You caught Gary and George with their pants down, you're good at this. A postmenopausal Sam Spade. It's the role of a lifetime."

I couldn't resist my own PR. Margo made a call. I was due at Felicia's Brentwood house at three. I wore the trench coat to get in character, a light rain legitimized my choice.

Women like Felicia Armstrong only exist in magazines. Poised, airbrushed, and ice-cold. I lost her at hello, I was not her kind of dame. I told her about Gary and me, and she thawed a bit. That's what I brought to the table or the empty bed. I knew how she felt, and I could provide what she most wanted and feared—the truth. For seventy-five dollars an hour plus expenses.

Felicia told me the basis for her suspicions. Taking his phone calls in another room, business dinners that went on too long, all-night poker games. And there was money missing from their substantial bank accounts. She didn't want to believe Mike was cheating, but now she had to know for sure.

"Why now?" I asked.

"I'm pregnant." I took her manicured hand and told her I'd take the case.

Gary came over with some documents for me to sign. He sneered at the loft which made me like it. I asked about life with Ronald. He gave me the usual rant. He couldn't afford his own place, every dime he earned went for legal bills. He told me I better get a job.

I told him I already had one. "I'm a private detective. Thanks to your infidelity, I found my calling."

"Who in God's name would hire you?"

"I can't reveal my clients." The more he scoffed and ridiculed, the more indignant I became. "I'm a dick, get used to it!" I loved calling myself a dick, it drove Gary crazy. "Dick, dick, dick, dick." I pelted him with my new identity.

Hacker must have heard us fighting. As Gary was leaving, Hacker asked him if Billie the Dick was home. Now that's a good neighbor. Gary's visit so enraged me, I went out and bought some equipment to make my career choice official.

Under Cover is a spy shop with a diverse customer base.

Jealous spouses, working moms with new nannies, cops and robbers staying current. And pros like me. The owner, Zeke, has a military crew cut and persona. There were cameras and monitors everywhere. I caught a glimpse of my profile. I had a double chin. It wasn't the lighting, it was irrefutable. I looked at myself in every camera and monitor on display. My behavior alarmed Zeke who asked to see some ID.

I showed him my driver's license and was upset that he didn't question my birth date. "I look sixty-seven to you?" Zeke stood down. I was vain, not dangerous.

I remembered why I was there and asked to see a shotgun microphone. It was a foot long and allowed you to hear a conversation two hundred feet away. My enthusiasm unsettled Zeke, "Why do you need it?"

"I'm a private detective."

His incredulous stare turned into a smirk, he saw me for the sucker I was. I got every gadget he convinced me I needed. GPS tracker, voice-activated recorders, snake scope to see around corners, a high-def DVR plus a portable model for my surveillance vehicle. A purse with a hidden camera—here I offered resistance. I didn't like the color. We decided I'd dye it. By the time I was done, I owed him seven grand.

"Will you be paying by check or credit card?"

I headed for the door. "I'll be back in an hour."

I went to a pawn shop and sold my diamond engagement ring. I asked for twenty thousand and was offered eleven. It was flawed, like my marriage. I was paid in cash, which I stuffed in my underwear. I walked out without the ring I'd worn for thirty years. I felt sad and yet elated. I felt divorced.

I went back to Under Cover and fished money out of my panties and bra. Zeke's smirk turned into a suspicious stare. The sucker had confounded him. I popped the trunk of my Civic, and he loaded my purchases into my surveillance vehicle. Not sure what to make of me, he memorized my license plate as I drove off.

I went to Samy's Camera and bought a Nikon with a telephoto lens and a video camera with night vision. Hacker got me a deal on a fancy laptop that could connect to all my equipment. I was broke again, but I was in business.

Gary was outraged I cashed in my ring to buy "spy shit" instead of giving it to the lawyer. It wasn't just about the money, my naked finger was a betrayal. I realized he missed me. Or at least the life we had together. Things were turning around, I was the one who was moving on.

The loft was filled with technologically challenging spy shit. Hacker lent his assistance in exchange for my mediocre cooking. I put on an apron and dissected a chicken as Julia Child, which was actually Meryl Streep's indelible version of Julia. After winning her third Oscar for her indelible Margaret Thatcher, she said she understood the public's "Streep fatigue." No hubris and so smart, and unparalleled in her art. There aren't many women who are widely considered the best in the world at what they do. She makes me want to be a better dick.

I got myself a new front door and had my destiny stenciled on the frosted glass . . .

BILLIE RIDLEY

PRIVATE DETECTIVE

4
FALLING FOR MY PREY

There was a new man in my life. Mike Armstrong was a powerful, charismatic fifty-three. I googled him, read all the articles. He ran numbers as a kid. Made and lost his first million by the time he was twenty-one. A blue-eyed Jew with just the right amount of gray in his hair, womanizing, unattainable. My kind of guy.

I followed Mike's Porsche as he headed down Sunset. The sun was out, the top was down, pretty women turned his head. The older woman tailing him in the Civic was of no interest. He darted in and out of traffic, Mike was always in a hurry. I had a GPS tracker hidden under the Porsche in case I lost him.

We went past the Whisky where I had sung backup for my boyfriend's band. I was twenty-one and barely made and lost enough to pay my rent.

Mike drove to Beverly Hills. He parked the Porsche in the driveway of a graceful house he once shared with his first wife, Sarah. I parked down the street and adjusted the telephoto lens on my camera. Sarah was Mike's age and very attractive. Her expression suggested she wasn't over him. I snapped some pictures before they disappeared inside the house.

I pointed the shotgun mic at the window. I was able to pick up a little of their conversation about their son, Danny, who'd just turned twenty-one. He had not made and lost his fortune. He had

Asperger's syndrome and still lived at home. Mike and Sarah went to see Danny, who was swimming laps in the pool. I crept around to the backyard to observe them. Asperger's is a type of autism often associated with extreme intelligence. Felicia told me that Danny was very smart, but couldn't hold a job, so Mike supported him and Sarah. His generosity was a measure of his guilt.

Danny got out of the pool. Mike gave his nonresponsive son a hug. Sarah handed Danny a towel, which he draped over his shoulder like a terrycloth toga. "Friends, Romans, wealthy fathers, lend me your credit card so I can get a car."

Mike smiled. "How about a pony?"

Danny persisted. "I got my learner's permit, give me a lesson."

"You're not ready."

"You said I could get a car when I was twenty-one. Lie to your wives, not your son." Danny went inside. Mike and Sarah had little left to say. I was glad I didn't have my camera, the picture was too sad. Mike got up to go, and I hurried back to the Civic.

Danny came out of the house in his toga and sat in Mike's Porsche. The drama made me forget how badly I had to pee. I turned on the shotgun mic. It was like a drive-in movie, all I needed was the popcorn. Mike came out of the house. Danny refused to get out the car until Mike gave him a driving lesson. Sarah watched from the doorway. Mike was a mensch, he didn't bully or belittle. He got in the passenger seat and tried to be a father. Danny could drive around the circular driveway all he wanted.

Danny did Dustin Hoffman in *Rain Man*. "I'm an excellent driver." Mike laughed, and the drama turned into a comedy. Also known as a dramedy. Which describes every movie I ever loved. They hardly make them anymore. My taste is becoming obsolete.

Mike went back to the office, then later that day, I followed him into the Hollywood Hills. He pulled up to an elegant house and checked himself in the mirror before getting out of the car. He pressed the intercom and announced himself.

Amanda Baron opened the door! A genuine movie star, still gorgeous, but like most actresses over forty, disappearing from the screen. I took some pictures, then they went inside. I called Margo, her Hollywood knowledge is encyclopedic. She said Mike was putting together the financing for Amanda's movie. She was less bankable these days, but Mike was loyal, she had been his first big client.

"And lover?" I inquired.

Margo wasn't sure. Amanda was famously married to Kip Cassidy, a pretty-boy actor who had been disfigured in a car accident ten years ago. Amanda pulled him from the car and saved his life. After reconstructive surgery, he looked okay with the right cameraman, but he hardly worked anymore.

Right on cue, Kip came home. The three of them were inside the house for over an hour. Mike and Kip came out together and got in the Porsche. Was this another Limber? I had such a crush by now, I didn't want Mike to be gay. I followed them to the Staples Center. They were going to a Laker game. Whoever Mike was sleeping with, it wasn't going to happen tonight. I was off the clock, time to go home.

I was at a stoplight when I saw Cleo Watson drive by—the big, black, hard-to-forget sister who stole my dining room set. Her check bounced. I hated getting screwed by someone I liked. I wasn't an easy mark anymore. I was Bogart. Tires squealed as I gunned the Civic and followed her fraudulent ass to Crenshaw.

I peered in the window of her well-kept house. She seemed to be alone. I banged on the door, which she opened wide. She acted like she was happy to see me. We sat at *my* dining table, and she told me her story over coffee and doughnuts.

"That check wasn't bad when I wrote it. I lost my job. Then my good-for-nothin' man cleaned out my savings." I ate a doughnut as she continued. "I was gonna find you, soon as I had the money. Jobs are hard to come by just now."

"What was the job you lost?" I asked, as the glaze melted in my mouth.

"I worked for a plumber, he went out of business."

"Doing what?"

"Answering phones, snaking a drain, whatever was needed."

I didn't know how much to believe so I let her know who she was dealing with. "I'm a private detective." Then I asked for a glass of milk. She offered to work off the money she owed me at ten dollars an hour. I insisted on fifteen. So much for my Bogart. But I was lonely, and best of all, I would have an assistant named Watson.

I went home happy and made some notes on the case. The backup beepers and blinking BADA BANG didn't bother me as much. I wondered which came first, Tony Soprano's strip club, Bada Bing, or the seedy bar across the street. Harpo was rocking out, but I liked his music and felt no need to bang on the pipes. I took a rusty shower and sang along.

I went to bed with Scotch tape across my eleven lines. Mike had awakened my interest in men. What if I had a boyfriend? I couldn't tape my brow at night. But if I didn't, I'd have those ugly eleven lines and lose him. To tape or not to tape?

Beep, beep, beep. I absorbed the noise like the New Yorker I used to be and went to sleep. Harpo provided the score to my dream—I was dancing with Bogart who wore a fedora and trench coat. It was misty, like the end of *Casablanca*. He kissed me, and then he flew away in his Porsche.

Watson arrived early the next morning. She walked in and looked around. "You live like this?"

"I'm subletting the loft from my nephew, Stella." Watson gave me a say-what look. Stella was best explained by his closet, which Watson embraced by wrapping a feather boa around her neck. I put on a wig to wear to work in case Mike had spotted me.

June called. I told her to talk to my assistant who would be taking her to the doctor. Watson finally got off the phone with my mother. "I'm gonna need a raise."

I took her to June's apartment and showed her how to dispense the meds. They were like Laurel and Hardy. Watson was twice her size and my shrunken mother was addled by age.

"Why you wearing all that paint?"

"I'm not dead yet. I try to remain attractive."

"From fifty feet away?"

Watson took charge, I was no longer needed. "Go do your detecting. I got momma covered." I smiled all day thinking of Watson and June squaring off.

34

Mike had lunch at Nate 'n Al's deli. I was at the next table, in wig and sunglasses, with my back to Mike and his client, Norman Kaufman. Men tend to share their extramarital adventures, but today it was all about Norman's career. A short, frail, nervous wreck, he won Best Director his first time at bat. He'd been striking out ever since. The aging wunderkind was about to shoot an action flick in Vegas. Mike ate his pastrami on rye and listened to Norman's self-annihilating stream of consciousness.

"I'm creatively bankrupt, I have nothing to say, all I know is what I see in the movies. I have no opinions, no values, if I had any substance I'd kill myself."

"You won an Oscar, for God's sake. Pass me the mustard."

"What if they fire me, I'll never work again. You know better than me how broke I am, I'm going to lose the house."

"Let me have the key while you're gone."

"Just remember to change the sheets," Norman said resentfully.

So Mike did his cheating at Norman's place. I finally had a lead. I gave the waitress a big tip and left before he saw me.

I had Margo make a few calls. Norman was going on location the next day. The house was in the Hollywood Hills, right around the corner from Amanda Baron's house. Some silent film star had a big estate that was sold in parcels, and Mike bought them for his clients. The properties had doubled in value since then.

I followed Mike back to his office and knocked off when he went home to his wife. He worked long hours. Watson was gone by the time I got back to the loft. It looked a lot neater, the toilet no longer exploded, and I hadn't heard from my mother all day. I made myself something to eat, she also got the stove to light. Watson was indispensible.

I fell into bed. The backup beeper and blinking Bada Bang on my wall no longer bothered me. Beep, beep, blink, blink. I went right to sleep.

Watson arrived in the morning with coffee and doughnuts, and a carton of milk for me. Hacker smelled breakfast and came over. They were already pals, I was the third wheel. Watson called the phone company, I needed to get a landline for her to answer. We debated the greeting—"Billie Ridley, private detective." "Billie the

Dick." We settled on "Billie Ridley." People knew what I did, that's why they were calling. Hacker showed me how to use my video camera and I was off to my first stakeout.

Norman Kaufman's house was a sprawling eyesore in a rich and famous hood. Unpaid gardeners and handymen had abandoned him. I had been parked down the street for several hours. I brought a pot to piss in and all the popcorn I could eat.

Dr. Oz recommends Trader Joe's Organic Popcorn with Olive Oil. It comes in a metallic bag to keep it fresh and only costs $1.99. I sneak it into the movies and save a fortune. Dr. Oz is such an anomaly, a handsome, intelligent, trustworthy man. I wonder what he's like in bed. He's a heart surgeon who fixes hearts and doesn't break them. You wouldn't catch Dr. Oz at Norman's place.

At eight-thirty Mike pulled into the driveway. Ten minutes later the blonde pulled up in a two-door Mercedes convertible—in my day we called it a mistress mobile. In LA your sexuality is defined by your ride. There was Mike's powerful Porsche and her sultry Mercedes. And there I was in my secondhand Civic looking on.

The blonde fixed her exquisite face and headed inside. She had a runway walk, hair and hips swinging in tandem. Long sculpted legs, gravity-defying tits and ass.

My hands shook as I set the night vision on the video camera. I crept around to the side of the house and peered in the living room window. Norman's Oscar was on the mantle. Mike's jacket was on a chair, his cigar in an ashtray. I made my way to the overgrown backyard. The pool was filled with debris from the neighboring hillside. I followed the moaning and looked in the window. I found the smoking bed.

Mike Armstrong was a stallion. This wasn't Viagra, this was a fireball from the Bronx who'd made it big. Very big indeed. The blonde was wearing Jimmy Choo pumps and nothing else. I turned on the camera and hoped the lens wouldn't fog up. I've never been into porn—the hotter it got the more embarrassed I was. I looked away and let the camera be the voyeur.

I heard a noise coming from the backyard. Then I heard footsteps. *Holy shit!* I got out of there as fast as my flabby thighs could carry me. There was a parking ticket on my car. I fumbled frantically for my keys and sped off into the night.

I gave Hacker the license plate number on the blonde's Mercedes, and he hacked into the DMV. Her name was Jessica Kent. The car was new and registered in her name. Intrigued by her picture in *Maxim*, he hacked some more. Jessica was a model who wanted to act. She grew up in Fresno and moved to LA right out of high school. She recently purchased a townhouse that she was renovating. He got me an address. At his request, I compensated Hacker with a homemade meatloaf.

Watson lived up to her name and assisted me with my case. I gave her the backstory and we sat down to watch the steamy "sex tape," as it came to be called.

"It's hard to make a black woman blush," was her review.

The X-rated tape ended abruptly. I explained I heard footsteps and took off. "Maybe it was just a coyote. Or a security guard or a cop. I wasn't going to hang around and find out. What I was doing was very illegal."

I told her about the parking ticket. We agreed it was not a legitimate expense. Which brought up the subject of my client. "Felicia is pregnant with Mike's child. I can't show her the sex tape. It's too rough."

"You have to show her, that's what she's paying for," Watson argued.

"I've been the betrayed wife who saw too much. Visions of Gary still fuck in my head. Felicia needs to know he's cheating, she doesn't need the blow-by-blow. I'll go back and get some tasteful stills of a kiss." I loved the back-and-forth with Watson. But it was my name on the door and my decision. And so I resumed my stakeout.

I had been watching Norman's house for hours. Stakeouts can be very fattening. Cold pizza, warm smoothies. I could barely fit in the Civic. I threw on my wig and went for a walk. I got to the end of the sloping hill and saw Franky McVery jogging out of his rock star home. Franky was as big as the Stones in the '60s. I was all hair and boobs, dancing behind him on a TV show called *Hullabaloo*. After the taping, he said in his irresistible Irish rasp, "Nice jugs."

The hits just keep on coming. He still makes a fortune touring and marries models and has more kids. I sang a bar of his signature golden oldie as he ran by me. He flashed a sweaty smile. "Those were the days, darlin'." The man was an eternal stud. I went back to the Civic and found some classic Franky on the radio.

It was after eight when Mike pulled into Norman's driveway. I grabbed my Nikon and waited. Then *Amanda Baron* arrived. There was another other woman.

I crept around to the side of the house and peered into the living room. The windows were closed, so I couldn't hear them. It was like watching a silent movie, Amanda was so dramatic. They had a passionate fight, she slapped him, then they kissed. I got some pictures of the kiss, and they headed for the bedroom. I had seen that X-rated movie before and didn't need to shoot another one. I was pissed off. It was like Mike had been cheating on me.

I talked it over with Watson and she agreed, I needed to put the two affairs in context before reporting to Felicia. There was another reason I didn't want to wrap up the case, one I couldn't share. Investigating Mike Armstrong had become an obsession. I wasn't ready to let go. Mike was a dead ringer for my father. Except he was taller and had more hair. But they were both New York—different boroughs, same pastrami on rye.

The next day, I was waiting for Mike outside the deli. He pulled out of the parking lot and I followed him as he drove off. I put in a CD of Franky McVery's greatest hits and filled my mind with him. I pictured a bunch of middle-aged women taking off their practical panties and throwing them at the stage. I was deep in thought about another man, any other man, trying to wean myself from Mike.

A dog ran into the street, and Mike came to a screeching stop. I slammed on my brakes, but it was too late. I ran into the Porsche.

5
UP CLOSE AND PERSONAL

I was frantic, out of my mind. I finally got out of my car. "I hope that dog has a good lawyer," Mike said. I had to give him my real name, it was on my driver's license. Mike smiled. "I have every song Billie Holiday ever recorded." And he had the decency to be surprised at my age.

A Porsche's engine is in the back. It would have to be towed. I was panicking about all the money the accident would cost. Mike said it was his fault, and he'd take care of everything, including my deductible. You can understand why I was in love.

Mike got his stuff out of the Porsche, and I gave him a ride to his office. There he was, sitting beside me. I was so nervous my hands were shaking, I clung to the steering wheel. His hands were big and strong, I yearned for him to cop a feel.

Mike thought I was looking at his watch. "It once belonged to Howard Hughes. The inscription says, 'All my love.' Nobody knows who it was from. Most people think it was Hepburn."

"I think it was from Howard. He wanted women to wonder who it was from when he took it off and put it by the bed."

"That's the best theory I've heard yet."

His approval gave me goose bumps. I was a terrible private detective. He was a *married man*. His *pregnant wife* was paying me to investigate him. I didn't like myself. Mike saw my tortured eleven lines and asked if it had to do with Howard.

"Were you one of those women?"

Dear God, I was old enough to have fucked Howard Hughes. I pretended not to be devastated. "Two-inch toenails turn me off." Mike laughed and I realized he was kidding. But the sting remained, I was being punished for my unprofessional, unclean thoughts.

"You're pretty enough to have turned his head," Mike said. I was giddy again. His cell phone rang. "Hi, honey." *Which honey?* "Sorry, Pam, I'm running late." *Who the hell is Pam?* "I was rear-ended by a lovely lady who's giving me a lift." Then, seductively, "I'll see you soon."

"Was that your wife?"

"My assistant."

"Oh," I said, casually. I imagined them humping in the copy room.

Our journey ended much too soon. I dropped Mike off at his office on Sunset. "I hope you rear-end me again sometime." He grabbed his stuff and walked inside the building. Nothing gets to me like a man walking away.

I drove off in a daze. Then I passed Sunset Plaza. Duty, and jealousy, required me to check out Jessica's townhouse. The renovation was almost complete on the reward for her sexual favors. I couldn't *give* my sexual favors away, not even to my husband. I was convinced I'd never have sex again. I was headed for the nearest pint of ice cream when my phone rang. It was Mike. He left something in my car, a slim manila folder. I hung up and began to search. I found it wedged between the seats. In my exuberance I kissed the folder, then desperately tried to erase the frosted peach outline of my lust.

I sat in his reception area clutching my excuse to see him again. The predictably pretty Pam was relieved to see I was twice her age. "Right this way, Billie." Mike's enormous office had a view of the downtown skyline. He was sitting at his enormous desk. He smiled when I walked in.

"Can I get you anything?" Pam asked.

"I'd love a cup of coffee."

Pam left. Mike and I were alone. "You look familiar to me," he said.

"We met about an hour ago. I ran into your car."

"I could swear I've seen you before today. Were you ever a brunette?"

"Occasionally. I used to be an actress." Clearly he had some peripheral awareness of the novice detective on his tail, but he seemed to buy my cover.

"I like you better as a redhead."

"Red is my natural color." Thank God I wasn't wearing a wig.

"My mother was Irish, I have a thing for redheads." My heart was pounding out of my chest. His phone rang. "I have to take this, it's my wife." He picked up the phone. "Hi, honey." The windows were sealed, or I would have jumped. "The Morgan Stanley guys are in town, I have to take them to dinner." His silence suggested Felicia wasn't happy. Mercifully, he never mentioned me, but the call was sobering. She was his wife and *my client*. I was contrite.

Pam returned with my coffee and a distraction—Danny burst into the office wearing a T-shirt that said "Mike Armstrong Makes His Son Take the Bus."

Mike introduced us. "Billie, this is my son, Danny."

Danny ignored me. "I'm wearing this everywhere I go until you get me a car."

Pam tried to divert Danny's attention. "Can I get you anything?"

"A Coke and a Corvette," Danny said dismissively. He didn't like the women in Mike's life. There was an argument about the car. Danny became so agitated he defeated his cause. In lieu of transportation, he demanded a printer.

"You have a printer," Mike said.

"Yours is better. The color has to be precise. I want to send copies of my paintings to galleries so I can make a lot of money and buy a car!"

Mike pointed to a painting on the wall behind me. "My impossible son is an artist." He certainly was. It was a portrait of Mike that captured him completely. In the background was a small figure standing in his shadow. Father and son.

"You're really good," I said sincerely. Danny ignored me.

Pam tried to calm Danny. "I'll order you a new printer."

"I want his!"

Mike looked out the window. Asperger's made people hard to read. Danny misinterpreted anguish for disinterest. "Am I boring you?!"

"You're going to give me a heart attack."

"Is the printer in your will?"

Mike relented. "Take the printer." Danny disconnected the cables. Mike looked at me and shrugged.

"He's very talented," I said sympathetically. I knew what it was like to have a kid you didn't know how to help. Danny picked up the bulky printer and held it in his arms.

"Shall I call you a cab? How did you get here?" Pam asked.

Danny referred to his T-shirt. "Can't you read?"

"Where do you live?" I asked Danny.

"Beverly Hills."

"That's where I'm headed." I thought talking to Mike's son might be revealing.

Mike tried to spare me. "That's asking too much."

"You didn't ask, I volunteered."

Danny no longer ignored me. "Come on, Billie, we're out of here."

Danny was already out the door when Mike hugged me good-bye. It was fast, but heartfelt. "I'm glad we met." I can still feel his arms around me, even after all this time.

Danny got in my car. "You're too old for him," was the first thing he said. His insight made it hard to pump him about Mike. He wanted a driving lesson. "I'm an excellent driver," he informed me repeatedly. When we arrived at his house, I let him drive around and around in the circular driveway.

Sarah came out of the house and rescued me. "Judge Wapner is on TV." The *Rain Man* reference was her witty way of telling Danny to stop. I liked her already. She invited me in for a cup of tea. We sat in the kitchen, a kitchen that used to be Mike's. I felt more intrusive invading his married past than I did watching him have sex. Danny hovered in the background, protecting his mother from the guilty stranger.

"How do you know Mike?" Sarah asked.

I was chatty and reassuring. "He stopped short and I ran into his car. Why do they put a Porsche's engine in the back? I gave him a ride to his office, and he left something in my car, I was returning it when I met Danny and here we are."

Danny didn't believe me. "You acted like you were friends."

"He's paying my deductible. I love the guy."

I was old and affable. Danny didn't have to stay on guard. "I'll be in my studio." He grabbed a soda and left us alone.

Sarah felt the need to explain to her son. "The studio is where he paints. It used to be Mike's office. Danny took it over when Mike moved out."

The house was filled with Danny's paintings. There was one of Sarah that hung in the kitchen. She was standing at the stove and a young Danny was sitting at the kitchen table. Mike was represented by a place setting and an empty chair.

Sarah saw me staring at the painting. "Danny did that when he was just a kid. What he can't put into words, he paints. He has Asperger's syndrome. An amazing mind with no social compass. Mike couldn't handle it. He used to say, 'Our son is broken.'"

"I'm sorry," I said and meant it.

"The divorce was really hard on Danny. He's been angry at Mike ever since." She sipped her tea. "You have any kids?"

Since she was so open, I was too. "A daughter who has no idea who she is or what she wants. I feel like every mistake she makes is my fault."

"What about her father?"

"We're in mid-divorce. Be careful who you have a kid with."

"How long were you married?"

"Thirty years. How about you?"

"Nineteen. Mike loved me, he just couldn't keep his pants on. We're still pretty close. You met him, he's hard to hate."

"Gary's pretty easy to hate."

Sarah invited me to stay for lunch. She was an incredible cook, smart, funny, honest.

"What does it take to keep a man?" I wondered aloud.

"Firm thighs," Sarah said as she broke out the gelato. I genuinely liked this woman. I had already crossed so many lines I couldn't remember where they were. Mike's ex-wife was becoming a friend.

When I returned to the loft I told Watson about my highly unprofessional day. Rear-ending the man I was hired to investigate, driving in circles with his son, lunching with his ex.

Watson shook her head. "You don't know dick about being a dick."

I had to get back on the job. Mike knew what I looked like, so I raided Stella's closet in search of a disguise. I went with the Beyonce wig and hoop earrings. I found some of Gary's self-tanner and applied it to my sallow skin. I gave myself smoky eyes and thick brows. I looked like Groucho as a hooker. I tried to counter that with conservative clothing—a Church Lady dress and sensible shoes. I looked like an elderly hooker. I forgot about the green dye I put in the self-tanner to punish Gary. I looked like an elderly hooker from Mars.

Emma came by unexpectedly, she had been out of town, shooting a pilot. This was her first visit to the loft. "Hello, I must be going?" came out as a question when Watson opened the door. They had never met. Watson explained she was my assistant. I came out of the bathroom. Emma looked at me suspiciously. "Who are you?" If my own child didn't recognize me, Mike certainly wouldn't.

"It's me!" I said.

Emma backed away. "Daddy said he was worried about you, but I had no idea."

"I'm fine, honey, I just need to refine my disguise."

She gestured to my occupation stenciled on the door. "This is insane." Emma looked at me imploringly. "You need a shrink. Please, promise me. I'll pay."

"You don't have to pay. I have a case," I said defensively.

"Do you even know how crazy that sounds?"

She reminded me of Gary and I lost it. "Mommy is a dick!" Emma crumbled. I felt like shit. Nothing upsets me more than lashing out at my kid. Which is how Emma won most of our battles. I was an aggressive-passive. "I'll call my shrink, I promise." I was as motherly as I could be. "Would you like something to eat?"

Emma declined, she was on a diet. Then she devoured a peanut butter and jelly sandwich as she trashed her pilot. "It's another *Hoarders and Tiaras* atrocity that signifies the end of civilization." I listened to her rant, as did Watson, who saw my family as part of the job. When Emma paused for a sip of milk, I changed the subject.

"Your birthday falls on Thanksgiving this year."

"I'm used to sharing my birthday with a turkey."

Watson could relate. "I had a kid born on the Fourth of July. When he was little he thought all the fireworks were for him."

Emma was warming up to Watson. "How many kids do you have?"

"Two boys. One's in college and one's in jail. Different daddies, different outcomes."

Emma looked at me. "Watson is a find." Indeed she was.

When Emma left, I secured my wig and went to work. Mike knew my car, so Watson let me use hers. It was a battered Mustang she inherited from her ex. I thought about her carting my mother to doctors in this unlikely vehicle. June plays Miss Daisy and sits in the back seat.

Mike left the office very late. I followed him to a strip club on Sunset, The Velvet Swing. I was disappointed in him. When these girls were growing up they didn't dream of a handsome prince sticking dollar bills between their tits. Mike drove to the far end of the parking lot. He just sat there in his car.

I was parked on the street in the Mustang. A drunk tapped on my window, attracted by my Beyonce wig. "How much, honey?" I rolled down the window to give him a better view of my disguise. Elderly Martians were not his thing. "Never mind," he said as he retreated.

Ten minutes later a skinny guy on a Harley rode into the parking lot. He pulled up next to Mike's Porsche and got inside. By the time I got out my shotgun mic, the skinny guy was out of the car. He jumped on his bike and rode off. I had no idea what I had witnessed. At least Mike hadn't come here for the strippers.

I followed Mike home and called it a night. I was heading downtown when I noticed the black Lexus in my rearview mirror. There was a black Lexus in the parking lot at the strip club. I slowed down and let the Lexus pass me. The windows were tinted so I couldn't see the driver. He made a right on Vine and disappeared.

The next morning, I told Watson about my B-movie adventure—the mysterious guy on the Harley, the phantom Lexus. The drunk was her favorite part of the story. Emma phoned and reminded me of my promise to see a shrink. True to my word, I called Dr. Krasny. It was comforting just to hear his voice.

I sat in his office not knowing where to begin. Krasny asked me how I had been. This triggered an emotional avalanche. "I wasn't crazy, Gary was cheating on me, we're getting a divorce. The company went under, and I was broke, which is why I didn't call you. Now I have a new career. I'm a dick. I've taken penis envy to a whole new level—I simply became one."

"I never thought you were crazy." Krasny said. My tears dried up, and I returned his smile. "Tell me about being a dick."

"It's sort of like acting. I wear disguises, make up stories, after all those years of doing improv, I'm pretty good at it."

Krasny found my response insufficient. He suggested that looking into other people's lives and feelings was a way to avoid my own.

"I'm not avoiding my feelings. They're getting in the way. I have a crush on the guy I'm supposed to investigate. It's so wrong. His pregnant wife is my client." I was welling up with guilt. "He sleeps with models and movie stars, why would he want me? The upside is, my crush got me over Gary. I only love what I can't have. Like every other asshole who wanders in here."

"Maybe you'll wander out of here learning to love someone who can love you back."

I looked at my watch. "Forty-five minutes of spilling my guts for the bargain price of two hundred bucks."

"Anger is a good start," Krasny said. He was right. I felt better by the time I got home.

I had to wrap up Mike's case, my conscience couldn't take anymore. Felicia said he had a "business dinner" and would be home late. I assumed that meant a hot date at Norman's. I raided Stella's closet and selected a disguise—a long dark-haired wig parted in the middle, crystal earrings and a gauzy Indian shirt.

I got out my amazing Shu Uemura eyelash curler that all the makeup artists use. I curled my lashes in three different places—base, middle, and tips. My skin might be sagging but my lashes were forever erect. Mascara and liner to darken my eyes, a terracotta bronzer and no lips. I looked nothing like myself.

I borrowed Watson's Mustang and headed for Norman's place. Franky McVery was having a party, so I had to park up the hill. It was after nine and still no Mike. I watched all the rockers flocking to Franky's and listened to them jamming. I was hungry and needed to pee. So I crashed the party.

It was a rock 'n' roll crowd that spanned generations, many were Franky's contemporaries. I was not the oldest one there, just the oldest woman. The house was very grand, but cluttered with toys and musical instruments. There was a painting of Franky that got my attention. He was bare-chested in red leather pants singing to an auditorium of screaming old ladies. I recognized the artist. It was Danny.

Franky was late to his own party. When he finally arrived, he was disheveled and preoccupied. His live-in girlfriend accused him of being with her replacement. When he didn't deny it, she threw a bong in his direction. The watery brown residue splattered on the painting. Life accentuating art. His adorable four-year-old son came down the stairs to say good night to Daddy. Franky scooped him up and carried the boy to bed. Every time Franky felt old, he had another kid. Mummy was his fifth ex-wife.

I'm a rockaholic and some legendary musicians were playing the soundtrack of my youth. Music and weed wafted through the house. I was standing at the buffet table, stuffing food in my purse when an old rocker sidled up to me. He offered me a joint and called me "Rita." I guess it was the wig. He said I reminded him of Rita Coolidge. She was the sultry "Delta Lady" on Joe Cocker's

Mad Dogs and Englishmen. A lot of rockers have been in love with her, including the one handing me a joint. For one brief shining party, I got to be Rita.

I got so stoned I lost track of time. When I staggered back to my post, Mike's car was parked in Norman's driveway. I had been gone over an hour. It was hard to concentrate. I decided I needed to eat something. I dug the stolen food out of my purse. Olive bread, brie, *cupcakes*. The best thing I ever had in my mouth. I ate myself into a stupor.

Jessica pulled up in the Mercedes. She primped a bit and started toward the house. I took some pictures of her arrival, then I got out of the Mustang with the camera. All I needed was some stills of a kiss, and I'd be off the case. A grateful Felicia would recommend me to her wealthy friends. And Mike Armstrong would be out of my life.

Be careful what you wish for.

Jessica screamed and came running out of the house. She was hysterical. "Somebody help me!" She tripped and fell on the pavement, skinning her knees. There was a man walking his dog and two guys leaving Franky's party. They ran over to help her. One guy went into the house. I was reeling with fear. I heard someone say, "Call 911."

I don't know why but I had to see for myself. I went inside the house. He was lying on the living room floor. There was a pool of blood around his head. Mike was dead. There are some moments you spend the rest of your life trying to forget.

6

I DON'T DO DEATH

Somehow I got back to the Mustang. I wiped away the tracks of mascara running down my face only to produce another set. I heard sirens. Several police cars pulled up. There was a crowd by now, neighbors and people from the party. My car was blocked. I was still stoned, my head was spinning. I got out of the Mustang to get some air.

An unmarked police car pulled up and Detective Logan got out, a seasoned veteran who'd been on the job too long. Murder had become routine. He sent some cops to check out the crowd, then he went inside the house. One of the cops was heading up the hill. I was trying to get back in the Mustang when he caught up with me.

I started to panic—I was a semiprofessional private detective who was high on weed and obsessed with the victim. Everything about me suggested I was guilty of something. I decided not to lie, just avoid the truth. The cop was polite and to the point. I guess the Mustang looked out of place on the ritzy street. Or maybe it was my mascara-streaked face and glassy eyes.

"Is this your car?"

"Yes. No. It's mine tonight but normally not. I borrowed it."

He asked for my driver's license. He looked at me and then

back at the license. The picture looked nothing like my disguise.

"You look very different . . . Billie Ridley. Is this supposed to be you?"

The rocker from Franky's party saw me with a cop. "Stay cool, Rita. He's just some guy in a uniform who lost his humanity along the way."

The cop kept his focus on me. "Is your name Billie or Rita?"

"Billie." I took off the wig so I'd match my picture. "See."

The rocker reacted to my reveal. "You'll always be Rita to me."

The cop continued to press me. "So what were you doing here, Billie?"

"I was at Franky McVery's party." To give my story credibility I babbled about being a dancer on *Hullabaloo* when Franky appeared on the show. The cop had no idea what *Hullabaloo* was, having been born decades later.

But the rocker was a fan. "I jacked off to you every week." He was as taken with Billie as he had been with Rita. When the cop was able to get his attention, the rocker confirmed I was at the party. The cop took down all my information and walked off to question a neighbor.

The paparazzi began to arrive, chasing Franky and his guests back to his place. Franky had lost his strut. He looked fragile and frightened. He looked his age.

My enamored rocker grabbed his crotch as a salute to his teenage fantasy. "Too bad we didn't meet when I could get it up." Then he ran off, hoping to be photographed.

The cops kept the paparazzi at bay, making them turn their cars around. They made a big enough hole in the crowd for traffic to pass. I was able to make my getaway.

When I finally got home, I passed out. Every time I fell asleep some horrible dream would wake me. I'd remember Mike was dead all over again.

When Watson arrived the next morning, we sat on the mildewed couch and watched the news. Mike's murder was the lead story. There were clips of his famous clients expressing their shock and sorrow, including Amanda. I wondered who else knew the real reason for her remorse. Franky had regained his irreverence. "Mike Armstrong died like he lived—spectacularly."

The phone rang. I didn't want to talk to anyone. Watson covered for me. "Billie Ridley. I'm sorry, she's not here. I'll give her the message." She hung up. "That was your lawyer. The police have been asking about you." I sank deeper into the couch.

Margo arrived unannounced. Crisis management was her forte, and she was taking over. She pumped me as we watched the news. "Have you talked to Felicia?"

"I called her last night and left a message with the housekeeper. I don't know what to say. Mike's girlfriend found the body."

"I'm sure Felicia knows that by now. The police like to see how the spouse reacts."

We were interrupted by breaking news. The local anchor was ghoulishly excited. "The police believe Armstrong was bludgeoned to death with an Oscar. They found the murder weapon in the hills behind the house belonging to director, Norman Kaufman."

Margo stared at the TV. "This story will never go away. It's tabloid gold."

That's when I called Krasny. He could fit me in at noon. When I arrived, I told him everything that happened, then I went off on an internal tangent. "I've never been able to accept death. When my father died, I was too young to understand. I kept waiting for him. I still am."

"Maybe that's why you needed to go in the house and see Mike's body."

"I feel like it's my fault. I should have saved him."

"Is that how you felt about Murray?"

My tears were my unspoken yes. "I used to imagine him watching over me through a porthole in heaven. He's probably watching us right now."

"If you love someone and they die, they still live on in your heart. Your father will be here as long as you are."

I laughed it off. "I'm certainly getting my money's worth today."

"You're trying to distance. From me and your feelings."

"It's working." I couldn't stand to cry anymore or to love anyone. I circled back to death. "Here's the deal with getting old. Every week another friend gets some shitty diagnosis. I used to fall apart, but I've gotten so many of those calls, I take it in stride. I visit the hospital or take them to chemo and feel bad that I don't feel worse. My benchmarks are dropping like flies. I have a friend with cancer. She always got the guys. And I'm triumphant because she's bald, and I'll outlive her."

I wallowed in my guilt and went on. "I can only imagine what it's like for my mother. She's the only one left. Now that all her friends are dead, she's burying her doctors."

"Are you afraid of burying your doctor?"

"I wouldn't want to bury you. But I'd bury Gary." I looked at my watch and pulled my own plug. "Time's up."

"We have a few more minutes."

"Too many people leave me. I need to be the one who says when it's over." Krasny walked me to the door. "How can you let me go?" I said in mock protest. Except it wasn't so mock.

Krasny smiled. "I'll see you next week."

I was on my way home when Felicia called. I turned around and headed for Brentwood. There were news crews in front of the house. I rang the bell and Margo answered the door, she was there to handle the press. She parried with some reporters and let me in.

Felicia was stunningly unemotional. I was a wreck. Margo sat between us. "I'm so sorry," I said. Sorrier than she'd ever know.

"Tell me about my husband," Felicia said.

"Some of it is pretty hard to take." Her silence was my cue to continue. "You already know about Jessica."

"Was it serious?"

"It was expensive. He bought her a car and a townhouse." I didn't describe the X-rated sex. She knew they weren't playing chess. I worked up my nerve and went on. "He was seeing someone else."

Felicia seemed relieved. "That would imply he didn't love Jessica." Under that airbrushed facade beat the heart of a wife.

"She's one of his clients. Amanda Baron."

Felicia became so animated you could see actual lines in her face. "I thought that was over a long time ago. She was his mistress during his first marriage. When he left Sarah, it wasn't for Amanda, it was to marry me."

Margo tried to soften the blow with her own tale of marital woe. "At least he didn't leave you for a man."

"Mike didn't leave me. He died." Felicia made an attempt to open up and be one of the girls. "When a man is that good in bed, you pay the price of not being able to sustain his interest." It was a prelude to another question. "Was he sleeping with his assistant?"

"I don't know." I added gently, "Does it matter anymore?"

"It matters desperately to me." Then she took my breath away— "I want to hire you again." She paused to let it settle in. "I need to know who I was married to so I know what to tell my child about his father. The police may find out who killed him, but that's not enough. I need to know the truth. The other women, whatever you find." I managed a nod. Felicia never lost her composure. "He was brave and generous and deeply flawed. Many remarkable men are." Our eyes met and she quietly confessed, "I need to know if he loved me."

"I understand," I said. That was the rock-bottom question in any relationship. Husband and wife, parent and child, no matter how great the hurts along the way. I gave the widow her due. "I wonder if Mike knew how much he was loved." She offered me a thousand dollars a day plus expenses. The going rate for putting an unbearable loss in context.

7
A BIG FINALE

I needed a way to keep track of the players in Mike's complicated life. I went to Office Depot and got a large white erasable "murder board." You see them on cop shows, filled with pictures of suspects and relevant facts. Mine was on rollers and over eight feet wide. It could also function as a room divider in the loft. It went with my stenciled door and private detective decor.

I filled the board with headshots of the celebrities in the case—Amanda, Kip, Franky, and Norman. I used pictures I took of Sarah and Danny when I was tailing Mike. I found Pam's picture on Facebook and Jessica's picture in *Maxim*. I got a picture of Felicia from the society section. I had all the photos printed in the same 8×10 size.

In the center of the board was a picture of Mike. I took forever picking out the right shot. I chose a knowing smile—I figured Mike knew who killed him. Which one of the 8×10s was the last face he ever saw? Was he scared, did he see death coming? I stared at his picture and mourned. I missed this man that wasn't mine to miss.

Knowing who killed him and why would help me understand Mike, which is what I was hired to do. It was the detective in me, and the friend, I remembered him hugging me in his office. I had to know why he was gone. I had a new obsession.

I drew lines with an erasable black marking pen between Mike and the other pictures, making detailed notes about the relationships.

I added two more pictures to the board. One of a Harley and one of a Lexus. I drew a big black question mark on both pictures, and noted the date and location of each encounter. I called my two unidentified suspects "Harley" and "Lexus."

Watson and I studied the board. I drew arrows as I spoke. "Mike was sleeping with Amanda while he was married to Sarah. He finally left Sarah and married Felicia instead of his mistress." It was a familiar scenario. I nibbled on popcorn and thought out loud. "It reminds me of Onassis and Maria Callas, they had a passionate affair. But he blew her off and married Jackie Kennedy."

"It reminds me of Kanye and Kim. How many bitches did he dump for a piece of that famous ass?" Watson had a thing for Kanye.

I drew a diagram on the murder board of Norman's house relative to his neighbors. Franky was down the street, and Amanda was around the corner. They all had the same hillside as an extension of their property . . . the hillside where the cops found the Oscar used to kill Mike.

I jotted down notes about motive and opportunity. Amanda had a reason to kill Mike, and so did Kip, her cuckolded husband. Franky was an hour late to his own party and looked shook- up when he arrived. Norman was on location in Vegas, but they weren't shooting that day, one of the stunt guys blew up the set.

It was getting late, and Watson had to take my mother to the dentist in the morning. I scribbled some reminders on the board—"Pick up June's Vicodin. Get Stella's new address." Watson grabbed the marking pen and wrote—"Give Watson a raise."

She wanted to discuss our deal. "What happens when I work off my debt? I like busting husbands and figuring out who murdered Mike. Your momma ain't that hard to take because she ain't my momma, can't push my buttons if she didn't put them there."

We both knew I couldn't survive without her. "Consider the dining room set yours. I'll pay you seven hundred a week and more as the business grows." We sealed the deal with a pint of Rocky Road.

Watson is queen of the parting shots. "Lucky for you that check bounced." She grabbed the keys and headed home in the company Mustang.

I pondered the murder board for hours, making notes and erasing others. It was after three when I staggered to the bathroom and washed my face. I taped my eleven lines and fell into bed. The blinking Bada Bang shone on the glossy white board. A truck was backing up. Beep beep, blink blink. I was not in Beverly Hills anymore, nor did I want to be.

I was awakened the next morning by my door buzzer. I peered through the frosted glass at Rudy Logan, the detective in charge of Mike's case. I opened the door. Logan read the stenciled lettering. "Billie Ridley Private Detective." He flashed his badge and said in the same satirical tone, "Rudy Logan Homicide Detective."

Logan is tall with broad shoulders. A little overweight, but he wears it well. His sandy hair and scruffy beard are speckled with gray. I pegged him to be about sixty.

"I'd like to talk to you about Mike Armstrong," Logan said.

"Okay." I led him into the loft. I hate the way I look from the back so I walked sideways.

Logan stopped dead when he saw the murder board. "I don't know whether to laugh or arrest you." He turned back to the board. "How do you know all this?"

"Like it says on the door, I'm a private detective."

He asked a lot of questions, and I identified the primary players in Mike's life. "Who are Harley and Lexus?" I told him about observing Harley with Mike in The Velvet Swing parking lot and Lexus tailing me later that night.

Logan continued reading the board. "Who's June?"

"My mother."

"Who's Stella?"

"My nephew."

"Who's Watson?"

"My assistant."

"A detective with an assistant named Watson." He looked at me like I was nuts. "Where is Watson now?"

"She took June to the dentist."

"Watson is a woman?"

"That's right."

"But Stella is a man."

"He's a transvestite."

He was staring intently at my eyes. I held his gaze, I had nothing to hide. Then I realized he was staring at my eleven lines. I had forgotten to remove the Scotch tape. I was mortified. I peeled off the tape and tried to explain my unusual habit. "I can't afford Botox so I tape my eleven lines." Logan's converging eleven lines suggested he didn't understand. "I do it to avoid wrinkles." I was flustered and felt compelled to go on. "I used to be an actress, you pick up these little tricks."

Watson arrived in the nick of time. She could restore my credibility. "This is my assistant."

Logan was taken aback. "I thought you were imaginary."

Watson thought he was rude. "Who is this fool?"

Logan identified himself. "Detective Logan, LAPD. Can I see some ID?"

Watson gave him her driver's license. Logan looked up. "Your name is Watson."

"The Po-Po can read," Watson replied.

Logan's phone rang, he checked the number and took the call. "Yes, Captain. I'm still downtown. I can be there in twenty minutes."

"Was there a break in the case?" I asked. Silence. I gestured to the murder board. "Come on, Logan. I showed you mine, show me yours."

Logan was back where he began. "I still don't know whether to laugh or arrest you." He told me we weren't done and he'd be in touch. Then he took off.

I didn't have time to worry about Logan. I had to get ready for Mike's funeral. Some of the mourners knew me, so I needed a disguise. I chose a short brunette wig and a simple black dress. The makeup was minimal, I used waterproof mascara in anticipation of crying. I could disguise my appearance but not my grief.

By the time I arrived at Forest Lawn, it was standing room only inside the chapel. There were many tearful women, including me. I got in line to view the open casket. I was behind Pam, who was talking to the receptionist from Mike's office. They spoke in hushed tones, until Pam saw the body. "Why isn't he wearing his watch? He always wore his watch."

It was a good question. Where was his prized Howard Hughes watch with its anonymous *All My Love* inscription? Pam's reaction was telling. I suspected the watch had been by her bedside, it symbolized something important to her. I wondered if Mike was wearing the watch when he died. Did the killer take it as a trophy?

It was my turn to view what remained of Mike. His handsome face was in slack repose, his strong hands folded across his chest. I shut my eyes to stop the tears. I didn't want to remember him dead. I wanted to remember him defiantly alive, eating pastrami on rye, paying my deductible, breaking hearts, living each day like it was his last, until one of them finally was.

Before the service began, I moved around the periphery, observing the mourners. Norman had flown in from Vegas. A Studio Suit asked how he was doing. Norman was already unglued, this pushed him over the edge. "The set blew up, I have a drunken stunt coordinator and a star with bad hair, it's a hundred and twenty degrees in the shade, and I just lost my best friend."

Amanda was inconsolable. I gathered she had been sedated. She sobbed and then nodded off on her husband's shoulder. Kip poked her in the ribs. Amanda woke up and called him names, then she started crying again.

Franky's entourage included his former wives and litters of children, ranging in age from four to thirty. They all seemed to get along, united in their need to be in his orbit.

A lot of eyes were on Felicia. The widow was the only woman who did not shed a single tear. She sat next to her father, Oliver Whitney, CEO of all he surveyed. He was the portrait of disapproval, this was not his kind of crowd. I wondered if his contempt extended to Mike, the man who had betrayed his daughter. I had a new suspect. Whitney was going on the murder board.

Jessica was standing in the back of the chapel. The mistress wore no makeup and stayed in the shadows, her tears muted by the inappropriateness of her attendance.

Felicia looked back over her shoulder. She allowed herself an ice-cold glimpse of the other women grieving for her husband—myself among them, although in disguise. I looked for Jessica, but she had already gone.

Sarah and Danny sat on the other side of the aisle from Felicia. The two women exchanged a look of recognition. Each one knew how much the other had lost. Danny became very agitated. It was all he could do to stay in his seat. He stood up and sat down again. He could not escape a pain he didn't know how to express.

I spotted Detective Logan in the crowd, he wore a dark suit, trying to fit in. I watched him watching everybody else. My eyes followed his around the room, until they landed on mine. He looked at me a tad too long, either he was attracted to somber brunettes or I had been made.

Organ music was piped in and the service began. A nondenominational officiate said nice things about a man he didn't know. Then came the eulogies. Friends of Mike, or "FOMs," as they called themselves, made their way to the podium and told stories about him, each one attempting to outdo the other in eliciting laughter and tears.

Mike had a packed house. I'd be lucky to fill three pews. I needed to make more friends so they would come to my funeral. I would live a bigger life, give the FOBs great material. I hoped I would not die until I became as missed as Mike.

Franky was the biggest name on the bill and the last to speak. "Mike was my best friend. He was everybody's best friend. Best man at my weddings, Godfather to my kids. Mike was the man. Now the man is up there telling the Lord how to double his money." Franky cleared his throat, willing back tears. "It suits Mike that he was murdered, so naughty and noir. That's how I would like to go." He cautioned his ex-wives, "But not just yet." He got a laugh and went on. "Years ago I was rolling through France and got arrested for a having kilo of merriment. To ensure my freedom, Mike got my driver to marry the judge's daughter." Franky nodded, and the portly couple stood up and waved.

Franky's million-dollar voice cracked. "What will all of us do without our best friend?"

Danny suddenly stood up. Discomfort swept through the crowd as he headed for the podium. Franky gave the unanticipated speaker the floor. Danny avoided eye contact with anyone. He turned his head in the direction of Mike's casket. It took him forever to say anything.

Franky stood behind him, watching out for Mike's kid. "In your own time, boy."

Danny was too loud, then he spoke more softly. "He wasn't my best friend. He was my father. When I was young, people said I had his eyes. I used to think that was why he couldn't see me. I took everything literally. I still do. Now I want to see him. But he's not here. He's in a box. My mother says he's watching over me. But how can he do that if I have his eyes?" Danny left the podium. Franky walked him to his seat and stayed by his side.

What would Emma's eulogy be for me? Above all else, I am somebody's mother. With all my wounded heart, I wanted to get that right.

By the time I got home, my waterproof mascara was in sad little clumps. I added Oliver Whitney's picture to the murder board. Number eighty-nine on Fortune's list of the egregiously rich. Watson called him "Whitey," and based on his Cheney face she decided he was guilty.

The phone rang. It was Logan. I had to go down to the station and give them a statement. I hung up and spun out. What would I say, what would I wear? This was my first official interrogation. It's something a dick never forgets.

8

THE OTHER MAN

Norman Kaufman was leaving the police station as I arrived. His cell phone trembled in his hand as he described his interrogation. "It was *Usual Suspects,* nobody believed me so why should I—I have trust issues from lying to myself. It turned into *Marathon Man,* I lost my shit and begged them not to pull my teeth." The paparazzi chased Norman to his limo and ignored me as I went inside.

Logan escorted me to a small, sterile room. There was a two-way mirror on one wall. I was being observed. I'd seen this scene a million times on TV, and now it was happening to me. We sat down on opposite sides of a metal table.

"Am I a suspect?"

"I don't know what you are," Logan replied.

I looked at the two-way mirror and waved. "I didn't do it." I covered my anxiety with shtick. "Are you taping this? The lighting sucks." I turned to Logan. "Can we switch chairs, this isn't my good side."

Logan tried not to laugh. "I saw you at the funeral. Why the wig?"

"Some of the suspects knew me."

The Bad Cop walked in. He was short and mean to Logan's tall and friendly. I looked at Logan. "You needed backup?"

The Bad Cop took a seat. "You claim to be a private detective?"

Logan added, "You can't just write it on the door. You need a license."

"I'm looking into it," I said.

"You'd never qualify," the Bad Cop informed me. "You need a background in law enforcement or six thousand hours working for an established investigator."

"It's a little late to join the force, and I don't have six thousand hours to waste."

"Exactly. You're too old for this line of work."

Logan intervened, "I think she gets the point."

The Bad Cop pressed on. "What was the nature of your relationship with Armstrong?"

"We didn't have a relationship."

He looked at my file. "You got a parking ticket that puts you at Norman Kaufman's house a week before the murder. You and Armstrong were involved in a traffic accident."

"I was tailing Mike and I ran into his car."

"Either you're the worst PI in the world or you're a liar." The Bad Cop bore down. "I think you were stalking him. What happened, Billie, did he lead you on and then dump you?"

"I'm flattered by the allegation, but Mike was out of my league."

"I could see you together," Logan said. The Good Cop was very good at his role.

The Bad Cop didn't let up. "Somebody saw you go inside the house after the body was discovered." He showed me a photograph of Mike's body with the pool of blood around his head. "Look familiar?"

I turned away. "Yes."

"Why did you go in there?" Logan asked.

"I don't know," I murmured.

The Bad Cop pounced. "Maybe you needed to retrieve some incriminating evidence."

I welled up remembering. "All I did was look at him, and then I left."

Logan grew suspicious. "You seem to be taking his death pretty hard."

The Bad Cop loomed over me. "Why were you wearing a wig and driving someone else's car?"

"I was on a stakeout, and Mike knew what I looked like."

"Stakeout—stalking. Call it whatever you want. You were obsessed with him."

That happened to be true, but my accuser was only guessing. "I was at Franky McVery's party when Mike was murdered."

"I thought you were on a stakeout."

"I took a little bathroom break."

"What time did Franky arrive?" Logan asked.

"I don't know exactly." I cleverly busted myself. "I was too wasted."

"So you admit to taking drugs?" the Bad Cop said.

I turned to the two-way mirror. "It was rock star weed, I was ripped out of my skull." Logan knew what I was doing, but I had to explain it to his partner. "If I was wasted, it implies I was at the party and didn't kill Mike. I have a witness who calls me "Rita," he can ID me if I wear the wig."

The Bad Cop was at a loss. Logan took the lead. "Who hired you?"

"I'm afraid I can't divulge my client."

The Bad Cop blew. "You don't even have a license. There's no privilege for some wacky amateur."

It was only a matter of time before they found the cancelled checks, still I felt awful giving her up. "Felicia Armstrong."

The divulging went on for another hour as I detailed what Logan had seen on the murder board. Every suspect, motive, and opportunity. When I was done, Logan defended me. "Pretty impressive for a wacky amateur." The Bad Cop had no response, which I took as a compliment. They told me not leave town and let me go.

I was too tired to face rush-hour traffic so I went to the coffee shop across the street. I collapsed into a booth and ordered chocolate cake, then I went to the ladies room.

When I came out, Logan was waiting for me. "Mind if I join you?"

"Do I have a choice?"

"It's me or jail." He ordered apple pie and asked the waitress about her kids. He was the Good Cop wherever he went. Logan sat there sizing me up.

"What?" I asked him.

"What?" he repeated.

We hardly knew each other, but there was familiarity in the exchange. I started to let down my guard. "Who was behind that two-way mirror?"

"Half the squad. I told them you were very entertaining." He had a great smile. "That was some show you put on."

Logan dug into his pie, I dug into my cake. We glanced at each other occasionally. It felt like a date. Suddenly I was worried about how I looked. The dick was turning into a girl.

"How did you become a private detective?" he asked. I was lost in thought. Detective Logan was a lot of man. I wondered what he was like in bed. "Billie?" I loved the way he said my name. The deep voice went with the broad shoulders. He was staring at me with those penetrating eyes. I realized I was supposed to speak.

"Yeah?"

"How did you become a private detective?"

"I busted my husband for cheating, then I busted my girlfriend's husband. Then I got hired by Felicia. Infidelity is my specialty."

"This is no longer infidelity. This is murder. You could get hurt."

He was protecting me. I love that in a man. I looked at his strong hands. There were scars on his knuckles. He was the real deal. "Did you ever kill anyone?"

"Twice."

"How do you get over that?"

"You don't." He wasn't used to revealing himself. We had switched roles, I was the interrogator.

"Do you like your job?"

"I like it right now." I returned his smile, and he revealed some more. "It's a strange way to spend your days, but somebody's got to do it. I've been at it way too long, but I can't bring myself to retire. I'd rather catch killers than play golf."

"How old are you?"

"Sixty-three. That's two hundred in cop years."

I had vowed never to lie about my age. "I'm sixty-seven," I proclaimed.

Logan looked up from his pie. "I know, I read your file."

My age didn't seem to repel him. He was only four years younger than me. Women outlive men by an average of seven years. Why is it always younger women with older men? The guy dies, and the wife has all those years alone. It should be older women with younger men, they'd kick off at the same time. Logan and I were a good match in terms of our mortality. We had a common passion for detection. And I liked the way he looked at me. He was a good guy.

So good that he volunteered he was married. I looked down, trying to hide my disappointment. I already had us living on his pension in a little house in the Valley. Solving murders on the weekends. Dying two months apart. "Why no ring?" I finally asked.

"So the bad guys don't go after my family."

I was embarrassed, I had to get out of there. "My mother is having root canal, I promised her a steak dinner while she could still chew." Logan pretended to believe my lie. I threw a five dollar bill on the table and stood up.

He returned my money. "I got this."

"Don't be silly, it's not like this was a date." I was so painfully obvious.

Logan picked up the check. "Please, Billie, allow me. Otherwise it's bribery—I let you off for a piece of pie. And some good company."

I drove home in a funk. I was the betrayed wife, not the other woman. I was still guilty about my crush on Mike. I would not do it again with Logan. The problem is, there are no available men, all the good ones are already taken. The bad ones are taken too.

My funk was interrupted by my paranoia. I saw a black Lexus. My heart raced as it pulled up beside me. The driver was an Asian housewife with a toddler in a car seat. Every time I went out I saw a black Lexus. They couldn't all be tailing me. And not every cup of coffee was a date. Get over yourself, reality said. As always, I ignored it.

When I got home, I stared at my stenciled door. Billie Ridley Private Detective had to get a license. Books and movies are filled with unlicensed sleuths. Nick and Nora Charles, Lisbeth Salander, Miss Marple. They wouldn't be stopped by something as trivial as documentation. But they were only fictional. I had the LAPD on my ass.

I considered calling myself a detection coach. I had a friend who was a life coach. No training, no degree, she just hung out a shingle. You can stick "coach" after anything and the state of California leaves you alone. I decided to give it more thought before redoing the door.

Watson had written "Call Felicia" on the murder board, along with June's shopping list—Velcro curlers, bananas, and Nexium. I returned Felicia's call and said I would be there first thing in the morning.

Felicia's father was not happy to see me. "Hello, Mr. Whitey," I said, intending to say "Whitney."

Felicia jumped in. "Father doesn't approve of what we are doing."

"Let sleeping dogs lie," he warned. Spoken like a man with something to hide.

We left Whitey behind and went to Mike's study. I updated Felicia and told her what I told the cops. I asked to see Mike's credit card receipts and cell phone bills.

"What are you looking for?

"Anything to help me fill in the blanks." We went through Mike's desk. There was a copy of his will. Felicia said Mike was amending it to include the baby. Danny's share of his father's estate would be cut in half.

"Did Danny know that?" I asked.

"Mike told him about the pregnancy. I assume he knew about the will." Felicia looked at the picture of Danny on Mike's desk. "He's such a troubled kid. I respect that he's Mike's son. But I'm afraid of Danny. Not for me, but for the baby." I tried to be reassuring, but Danny was hard to predict.

We found something in the desk that upset Felicia. It was the script for Amanda's movie, along with a budget. Amanda wasn't bankable, so Mike was putting up his own money. Felicia shut the door so she wouldn't be overheard. "I miss him so much. Then I get so angry. I don't know how to feel." She looked at me beseechingly. "His affair with Amanda lasted through both his marriages. If that isn't love, what is it? Why didn't he marry her, was it because of Kip? It's all I can think about."

Whitey walked in and Felicia withdrew. "I'm not feeling well." She went to the powder room in the foyer. We could hear her throwing up in the background.

"Morning sickness," I told her indifferent father. "It goes away soon." I continued to talk over the retching. It might be my only chance to question him. "Can you describe your relationship with Mike?

"Certainly not to you."

"Part of my job is to anticipate the questions of the police and the press. The more I know, the more helpful I can be. I'm trying to protect Felicia. And her family."

Whitey gave me a begrudging response. "Mike and I were involved in some business deals. That's how he met Felicia. I was opposed to the marriage. It brings me no pleasure to know I was right."

"I understand you have a home in Santa Barbara."

"And one in Connecticut and one in London."

"Which one were you in the night Mike was killed?"

"I was in Santa Barbara. I got a call from Felicia a little after midnight. She told me what happened, and I drove down to be with her."

"That's only a two-hour drive—"

Felicia walked in. Whitey complained to his daughter. "This ludicrous woman suspects me of killing your husband."

I kept my cool. "I won't be the only one asking where you were that night."

Whitey sneered. "I was at home. In bed. I was not alone. I believe that's all you need to know."

67

Felicia turned to me. "He was with his mistress. Just like my husband." A dam broke deep inside and she began to cry.

"Pull yourself together," her father said without sympathy.

"I'm a pregnant widow. Fuck propriety!" It was the first time I liked my client.

Whitey went wild. "You brought this on yourself. Your life with that man has been a disaster. Now this sordid business of a murder. I dine with heads of state. Your husband has reduced me to tabloid fodder!"

Felicia saw his outburst as a victory. "Pull yourself together," she said vindictively. Whitey walked out of the room and out of her house.

Felicia froze over again. "Women who marry men who cheat rarely have fathers that don't. He's always had other women. My mother seemed to accept it. I thought I could, but I was wrong."

"I doubt your mother could handle it either."

Felicia felt too exposed. She put me in my place by writing a check. We were not friends, I was an employee. She had the housekeeper show me out.

I went home and stared at the murder board. It had become a form of meditation. Watson and I discussed Whitey's alibi. He had plenty of time to kill Mike and get back to Santa Barbara to receive Felicia's phone call. Watson felt that no woman would share his bed without getting paid. And that kind of woman could also be paid to say she was in his bed when she wasn't. "Only a ho would lay down with Whitey." Having met him, I was inclined to agree.

I had Hacker investigate Whitey's financial dealings with Mike. As a cyber warrior for Occupy Wall Street, Hacker despised Oliver Whitney. Merging and acquiring, laying off workers, the poster boy for the one percent. He hacked into bank accounts and stock portfolios. Whitey and Mike had partnered on several investments, all of them overseas and hard to trace. There was an offshore account that was closed two days before Mike's murder. I wasn't sure what all that meant, but it kept Whitey in the running as a suspect.

I made Hacker an apple pie to thank him and ate two pieces myself. Every time I thought about Logan, I felt like I was betraying Mike, how crazy is that? Dead or alive, married or not, any unavailable man will do. Margo calls it "French pain." I was in love with longing.

9
IMMORTAL ME

Felicia made it clear that defining Mike's affair with Amanda should be my top priority. I was as curious as she was. Was Amanda Baron the love of his life or his killer?

I needed access. Margo found out that Amanda had mold and would have to redo her bedroom and bath. We went to see George and Limber in their happy new home. Margo told George to bid on Amanda's job just to get me in the door. "If it weren't for Billie, you'd still be married to me instead of blissfully contorting with Limber."

Two days later, I was standing in Amanda's bedroom. George introduced me as his assistant. No disguise was required, as an assistant I was nobody to Amanda. George did some sketches. He'd expand the closet, enlarge the balcony, redo the bathrooms. The palette would feature a violet blue to match Amanda's eyes. He left me behind to take measurements. I had to be there every day to accept deliveries and make sure Kip and Amanda were not inconvenienced.

And figure out their marriage. Understand Amanda's enduring affair with Mike. Find out if Kip knew about his wife's affair and determine if either of them was capable of murder.

They were both actors and high maintenance. It took a village to keep Amanda one of *People Magazine's* Most Beautiful. Before his disfiguring car accident, Kip had been a six-packing Pitt. Now he was a scarred reminder not to drive drunk.

Amanda had a movie that was premiering in a few days, and the red-carpet transformation had begun. She had Botox and fillers, all perfectly timed to reap maximum cosmetic benefit on the big day.

Her stylist arrived with a seamstress. A rack of designer gowns was wheeled in. It was the first time Amanda acknowledged my presence. She would try on a dress and have the household help and assembled nobodies vote on the most becoming. The workmen liked anything low-cut. Her stylist favored dresses hot off the runway, suggesting to Amanda it kept her more current, which is code for *young*.

The skintight Versace was the front-runner, until I said it didn't look good from behind. Suddenly, I had earned her trust. I had her backside. I was allowed into the guest bedroom, which had become Amanda's boudoir and cosmetic headquarters during the remodel. Kip had been banished to the maid's room, and the maid was sleeping in the pool house. Rosa, the displaced maid, said they often played revolving beds. "Miss Amanda don't let Mr. Kip sleep with her if he drink too much."

The stylist brought in a selection of designer shoes to go with the Valentino dress that was voted the winner. The pumps Amanda chose were too tight. The stylist went in the bathroom and filled the expensive shoes with hot water. I was horrified. The water was dumped out and Amanda put on the shoes. She walked around, trying on accessories, picking out a purse. Soon the shoes no longer hurt. They had conformed to the shape of her foot.

Learning this trick was worth my becoming a dick. I went home and poured hot water in the toe box of my painful shoes, being careful to keep the water on the *inside* only. Then I walked around in the pliable shoes until they fit my fat little foot like a glove.

Amanda's face was injected perfection but her eyes were puffy from crying, presumably over Mike. She would apply tiny bags of frozen peas to reduce the swelling, only to tearfully puff up again. I wondered how her husband felt about that.

In preparation for the red carpet, Kip was working out in their home gym. I went in with some trumped up question about his remodeled closet. He was standing on a giant vibrating plate used by athletes, movie stars, and most notably, Madonna. I thought the slurred words were because he was vibrating. I got close enough to smell his breath, he was drunk. Kip was happy to talk to me, he was often ignored and loved the attention. Between the slurring and the vibrating, he was difficult to understand.

"Amaaanda treeets meee liiike shiiit," Kip confided.

"I see." I wasn't sure what he said, so my responses were generic.

"Sheee ruuuined my liiife."

"Really."

"I couldaaa beeen a contenderrrr." Kip continued to pour his heart out, albeit unintelligibly. He even mentioned Miiike by name.

The personal trainer arrived. Gunther was a muscular man with a shaved head and no body hair. He coaxed Kip onto the Pilates machine. Kip did a few reps. "I don't know why I bother. Nobody's going to be looking at me when I'm standing next to Amanda. She'll hog all the interviews, they won't even ask me who I'm wearing." Kip went limp and let his limbs drop.

"Give me ten more, big guy," Gunther said.

Kip gave him four and looked over at me. "You've been very sweet, Bobbie."

"Billie. I'm George's assistant."

"How would you like a workout with Gunther?"

"Sure," I said. Kip closed his eyes and went to sleep on the Pilates machine. I got a free hour of Gunther. He had shaped a lot of famous bodies, and now he was molding mine.

Crunches were a waste of time. I was to do bicycles, lunges, and squats. And do them all the time. In the car, watching TV. Sucking in my core in public and private. Every flight of stairs was an opportunity to firm my thighs. "If you're not moving, you're dying" is one of Gunther's many mottos. Unused muscles send the body a signal to expire. If survival wasn't sufficient motive, he appealed to my vanity. "Sitting on your ass makes it spread."

"Walk it off." Not just the weight, you can walk off anger,

anxiety, depression. We pump stress hormones all day long. If you don't burn them off with physical activity, the cortisol and adrenaline build up and make you nuts. It doesn't have to be punishing. Just circle the block a few times. Strenuous cardio only makes you overeat. Gunther likes resistance training, lifting dumbbells builds muscle and bone. "Your flabby arms stop waving good-bye when you do."

When we were done, he gave me a copy of his DVD, *Get Moving with Gunther*. I move with him every day, as booty and mood continue their ascent.

Amanda came into the gym. Kip woke up and pretended to be stretching. She announced she was going out and Kip went back to sleep. Gunther summed up the relationship. "Sometimes walking it off isn't enough. You have to walk away."

Every afternoon Amanda would disappear for a couple of hours and come back looking vibrant and content. I wondered if she had a lover.

I went outside and hid in the Civic, waiting for Amanda. I followed her through Benedict Canyon to a pink castle. Only a woman could live here. Either Amanda was bisexual or her afternoon trysts were not with a lover. When Amanda was safely inside, I took a closer look. The house was regal in a frilly kind of way, with fountains and rose bushes, and a royal crest over the door. I opened the swan mailbox and found mail addressed to Olga Romanov.

I had heard of Olga, the famous nutritionist, but I needed to know more. I called Margo. She had actually gone to Olga a few times. "I'd rather decay than drink that green slime."

Olga emigrated to the US from Russia so long ago that Ava Gardner had been a client. She claims to be related to Anastasia— the one killed in the revolution, not the eyebrow expert. What Margo loves about Olga is her big mouth. She's a notorious gossip. Telling the secrets of Hollywood royalty makes her their equal, a member of the club.

Margo pulled some strings and got me an appointment with Olga so I could pump her about Amanda. And possibly develop a taste for green slime.

Who knew that investigating Mike's murder would double my life span.

Olga's gilded living room was filled with family heirlooms, a white Steinway, a dozen Faberge eggs. She had so many mirrors you couldn't avoid seeing yourself age. And so many clocks you couldn't forget time was running out.

The colon cleansing tea was served in a Limoges cup. I sat in an empire chair marveling at Olga. She had to be at least my age, but she looked infinitely younger. Her raven hair was pulled back in an elaborate bun. Her skin was supple and unlined. She wore no makeup, just red lipstick. She was ageless, timeless. The clocks and mirrors were her friends.

Olga took an inventory of my health habits. I mentioned Amanda casually, saying we had the same personal trainer. It was like pressing the GO button on her red mouth. Her thick Russian accent made everything sound dramatic. "My darling Amanda. She lost a dear friend, all that crying is dreadful for the delicate skin around the eyes. My tonics can only do so much. Many of my clients are crying over him."

"Mike Armstrong," I said knowingly.

She gossiped to a more educated ear. "You must admire Amanda for staying with Kip all these years. He was so handsome before the accident. A perfectly proportioned face, good from every angle."

Olga took me to her rococo kitchen. A crystal chandelier, gold-encrusted cabinetry . . . and several scientific instruments to measure and evaluate whatever Olga ate.

"Tell me, Billie, what is your favorite thing to eat?"

"Ice cream," I confessed.

She went to the freezer. "Chocolate, strawberry, or vanilla?"

"Chocolate." Of course.

Olga handed me a scoop of chocolate ice cream on a cone. "Take a great big lick and then repeat after me." I took a lick of the rich dark chocolate ice cream.

"Yum," Olga said.

"Yum," I repeated sincerely. I took another lick of ice cream.

"Cancer," Olga said.

"Cancer," I repeated. I took a less enthusiastic lick.

"Heart attack," Olga said.

"Heart attack," I repeated. I took a reluctant lick and Olga went in for the kill—

"Wrinkles."

I stopped licking. Her red mouth smiled. "Yum is fleeting, wrinkles are not." She put out her hand, and I surrendered the dripping ice cream cone like a child who had misbehaved.

"Never again," I swore.

Olga made her famous green drink. "You must use a *blender*. Not a juicer—it strips away the skin, the most precious part of fruits and vegetables." She extoled each ingredient as she tossed it in. "Use frozen *wild* blueberries, they are more potent. Very important for the brain. One-half cup of *organic* carrot juice. Always organic, everything organic."

"Always organic," I vowed.

"One-half red pepper for the vitamin C. A handful of spinach for the B vitamins." She became reverential. "And *kale*. The healthiest food on earth. It is both a leafy green and a cruciferous vegetable. You get better skin, better eyesight, it fights cancer, heart disease, everything your ice cream invites."

"Kale," I repeated robotically. I was under her organic spell.

She handed me a bouquet of kale to hold. "Use two large stalks, just the leaf, not the spine. The more bitter, the better. Bitter means more nutrients."

"Bitter is better," I repeated, smelling my odorless bouquet.

"One tablespoon of flax oil. You need fat in order to absorb the antioxidants. Flax contains omega-3s and estrogen—good for the bones, and the dryness down below. A few sprinkles of cinnamon and turmeric, and our elixir is done."

She flipped the switch on the blender and yelled at me over the noise. "*Raw* vegetables preserve the enzymes that are destroyed by cooking."

"*Raw*," I yelled, in celebration of enzymes.

Olga turned off the blender and poured the green drink into two goblets. "To long life and good skin." We clinked our goblets and drank. It was as bad as Margo said. One sip was all I could take. Olga tossed hers back in a few gulps. She tilted her ageless face toward the chandelier. "I eat what I preach and look at the result."

I took another swig and shuddered from the bitter taste.

"You just added another day to your life." Longevity took control of my hand as I tipped the goblet to my mouth. Olga cheered me on as I drank and shuddered. "Another week . . . another month . . . another sixty years if you drink this every day."

I emptied the goblet and Olga applauded. "You are on your way to immortality." My stomach grumbled. I was afraid to open my mouth, lest the elixir come pouring out. Olga spoke and I digested. "Nature may take its toll, but Mother Science is on your side. Most diseases will soon be cured or controlled with medication. Eat as I do in the meanwhile, and you could live to be one hundred and twenty."

"Wow," I belched.

"It's a race between science and your organs. The longer you live, the better your chances of living longer."

I was hooked. *One hundred and twenty.* I was middle-aged again. Olga had thrown me back into my second act. The clocks chimed and her next client arrived. I would bill Felicia for this session as an expense, then I would pay my own way. Olga charged two hundred dollars, the same as Krasny. Body and mind cost the same.

The green drink kicked in on the way home. I had incredible energy. I ran to Whole Foods to get kale like I used to run for ice cream. I worked out with Gunther's DVD, studied the murder board to wind down, went to bed and woke up younger.

I made a green drink for me and Watson. She took a sip and spit it out, it was perfectly executed, like the old Danny Thomas spit takes. Except the beverage was thick and green, so it had shades of *The Exorcist.* "That is some nasty shit." I was not as persuasive as Olga, nor did I provide the same unlined example. But I'd find a way to share my elixir. I did not want to be the world's oldest dick without Watson by my side.

10
BLOOD ON THE RED CARPET

It was the big day, and the red-carpet countdown had begun. Kip and Amanda went to get electro-stimulation treatments. This is what many stars do before a public appearance. A microcurrent is applied to the facial muscles, lifting and plumping them. I used the opportunity to snoop. I found a pendant hidden in Amanda's lingerie drawer that was inscribed "*M.*" It was from Mike. I held it in my hand, and then I put it on. I put on one of the rejected red-carpet dresses and looked at myself in the mirror. I looked envious. Then I looked panicked—Kip walked in and found me in Amanda's dress with her lover's pendant around my neck. "You better take that off, she's right behind me."

Kip went out and tried to delay Amanda. I took off the dress and the pendant. Amanda walked in and found me in my underwear. "What are you doing?" she demanded.

I wiped my forehead and fanned my face. "I stopped taking my hormones and I'm having hot flashes. The workmen are everywhere, this was the only empty room." Kip stood behind Amanda giving me two thumbs up for my performance.

They went outside and let me get dressed. Later, I saw them in the kitchen. The red-carpet tension was building. Amanda was throwing back a green drink, and Kip was throwing back Scotch.

Amanda's glam squad arrived. When she departed, Kip said to me, "'Hot flashes.' You're twice the actress she'll ever be."

I went to the bedroom and watched the glam squad at work. Hairdresser, spray-tanner, makeup artist, stylist, and their fluttering assistants. Occasionally, I'd fake a hot flash so I didn't lose credibility with Amanda. Most of the squad was male and gay, and didn't know what to make of my strange behavior.

After a debate with the stylist, which the hairdresser won, it was decided Amanda would wear her hair down, obscuring the million-dollar earrings borrowed from Neil Lane. There was a security guard posted in the hall to protect them. The hairdresser put in rows of extensions, doubling the length and width of Amanda's hair, then hot rollers to add height to the crown.

The makeup artist admired her electrically-stimulated Loretta Young cheekbones. He put shadow under her Lorettas and dabbed on Benefit Cha Cha Tint stain. He glued on little individual clumps of lashes to pad her own and applied a trio of mascaras to prime, lengthen, and volumize. Then eye shadow, highlighter and smudged liner.

"Blink twice if you can still move your lids," the stylist said, implying it was too much.

Amanda took a vote, even asking the guard in the hall. "The eyes have it," Amanda declared, batting her augmented lashes.

The seamstress sewed Amanda into the Valentino dress. Out came the hot rollers. On went the jewels. She was a red-carpet goddess.

Amanda walked over to me. She turned around and presented her posterior for my approval. It's absurd how important it made me feel. I carefully checked for saddlebags, bra bulge, fabric pucker, spray-tan stains, the placement and symmetry of the silicone butt enhancers tucked into her Spanx. "Perfect!" I announced. The glam squad applauded. Amanda shook her enhanced ass, and I faked a flash.

Kip entered in a well-tailored tux. "That's what you're wearing?" the stylist joked.

"Give us the room, guys." Kip said.

The glam squad picked up their tools and took off. I lingered outside the door, chatting up the uniformed guard. "How much did the earrings cost? . . . When did you move here from Jamaica?" But I was actually trying to eavesdrop on Kip and Amanda. They threw insults back and forth. He was a lush and she was a bitch. It was the same fight I had heard all week. Then it got interesting.

"Don't you dare cry over him," Kip said. *Him* had to be Mike.

"He was the only man I'll ever love." So why was she married to Kip?

"Blah, blah, blah. He's dead, honey. It's just you and me."

"I'm sick of your drinking and pawing me!"

"I'm sick of lying for you!" Kip roared.

Lying about what? Kip and Amanda were each other's alibis the night of the murder. Was that the lie Kip was telling? Amanda became my prime suspect. God, I loved that show, *Prime Suspect*. I've seen every episode. Helen Mirren plays an older female detective. And here I was with a prime suspect of my own.

The limo arrived and I scurried downstairs. Amanda was crying about crying off her makeup. The makeup artist jumped in the limo to do emergency repairs. Amanda was lying down in the back seat so she wouldn't wrinkle her dress. Kip lowered the window as the limo pulled away. "Hurray for Hollywood."

I jumped in the Civic and headed for the theater on Hollywood Boulevard. Margo was able to get me a ticket to the premiere. I never made it to the red carpet as an actress, but I got there as a dick. My wardrobe was stashed in the car. I raided Stella's closet and chose a sequined Bob Mackie gown. And a modified Dolly Parton wig, in case Amanda spotted me. Changing clothes in the car was not easy. I took side streets and pulled over occasionally to wriggle into the dress and fasten the wig into place.

I got to the theater just as the procession of limos started to pull up. There were five major stars in the cast, that's what it took to get a picture made. The cheering fans were behind barricades. I put my Jimmy Chooed foot on the red carpet. It was a Cinderella moment. I was in a sea of celebrities and I was awestruck.

One of my guiltiest pleasures is watching red-carpet arrivals on TV. All the actresses put their hand on their hip and pose for the photographers. No one was taking my picture, but I stood around with my hand on my hip. Margo walked right by me, she didn't recognize me in my glamorous disguise. When I let her know it was me, her hacking laugh started to draw attention.

"Stop it," I said. "I'm working a case."

"But you didn't have to go Dollywood," Margo hacked.

Who knew if I'd be on a red carpet again? I wanted to make the most of it. I didn't expect to learn a lot about my prime suspect, but it was a great excuse to fulfill a dream.

When a star arrived, a publicist would usher them down the gauntlet of reporters. Amanda and Kip stopped to talk to Randy Sanborn. He was one of those Ryan Seacrest wannabes you see hosting the pre-pre-awards shows.

Margo and I watched the interview from the sidelines. Kip was weaving in and out of the limelight. Amanda's drunken escort was being ignored.

Randy was dying to know, "Who are you wearing, Amanda?"

"Valentino," Amanda gushed.

"Turn around so we can see the back." Amanda turned around, and I had a little wave of pride. Randy asked about her shoes and her jewelry.

Kip interjected, "I'm wearing Tom Ford and no underwear, my jewels are going commando."

"Good to know," Randy said.

Amanda tried to salvage the interview. "I'm very proud of this film. It isn't often you get to work with a director of Marty's stature."

"Most of her directors are taller," Kip added.

Randy kept his microphone pointed at Amanda. "You give an incredible performance."

"A ruthless killer wasn't much of a stretch," Kip said.

Amanda began to disintegrate. "Why are you trying to destroy me?"

"I don't want to destroy you. I want equal time," Kip replied.

"I can't take any more of your drinking."

Kip leaned into the mic. "She makes me sleep in the maid's room. Without the maid."

Randy asked, "Are you two putting us on, or is this for real?"

Kip referred to Amanda's tears. "She's not that good an actress." He turned to Amanda. "It's nice to see you ruin your makeup over me instead of your lover."

Amanda wiped her face. "You're a day-player and a lousy lay, why waste my mascara on you?"

Camera crews were deserting other interviews to cover the fight. Kip did not disappoint. "Amanda is not forty-one, she's *forty-four* and on her second facelift." He faced his enraged wife. "Soon you will be as unemployable as me."

Amanda slugged Kip. Blood trickled from his asymmetrical nose onto the red carpet. It was the punch that launched a thousand flash bulbs. Astonished celebrities and their handlers were laughing. Margo was hacking. I split a seam and started shedding sequins. They delayed the screening for over an hour, the producers feared the movie would pale in comparison to the marital circus.

The bloody battle had a Hollywood ending. Kip and Amanda were hot again. Paparazzi camped outside their house. Clips from the interview were all over E! *Inside Edition* did a retrospective of the marriage. For the first time in years, they were the lead on *Access Hollywood*.

"Any publicity is good publicity and meltdowns are best of all," Margo said.

George's workmen had to park down the street to avoid the news crews. The tile guy was also an actor and saw it as an opportunity. He took off his shirt and posed for the paps as he mixed grout in the driveway. He would have been fired, but it's hard to find a good tile guy.

Kip and Amanda were in the guest bedroom continuing the brawl. I grabbed some fabric samples in case I was caught eavesdropping outside the door. The yelling reached a crescendo and Amanda wailed, "I want you out of this house!"

The bedroom door suddenly opened. I held up the fabric samples. "Do you prefer ecru or eggshell for the accent pillows on the bed?"

"Ecru," Amanda wept. She stormed down the hall in her jersey jumpsuit.

"You look great from the back," I offered weakly.

Kip moved out. He grabbed his laptop and a bottle of Scotch. "I'll be at the Beverly Regent writing a tell-all." He got in Amanda's puffy face. "And I mean fucking *all!*" Now that was a book I wanted to read.

I started staking out Kip's hotel. He got himself a bungalow and began writing his book. Kip knew what I looked like, so I wore a disguise—a streaked wig and a Donna Karan dress. It's a posh hotel and I wanted to fit in.

I spent a lot of time lurking by the pool. I'd wander past Kip's room and look in the window. I could see him typing away. The floor was covered with crumpled paper. He never went out, he just wrote and drank. Finally, he left the room to go to the bar.

The maid went in to clean the room. She threw the crumpled pieces of paper into a plastic garbage bag which went on her cart. She wheeled the cart to a dumpster behind the hotel. In my mangled Spanish, I offered her twenty dollars for the garbage. Apparently, I misspoke.

She said in her broken English, "I don't like to go with girls." She threw the garbage into the dumpster and hurried off.

You see people dumpster diving in movies, but it isn't so easy in real life. I was wearing a dress and heels. I hung my shoulder bag around my neck and scaled the wall. I perched on the ledge with the rim digging into my ass. I saw a janitor coming. I had no way to explain myself, so I dove in. He tossed a load of garbage in the dumpster, much of it landing on me.

I dug around, looking for the crumpled paper from Kip's room. I found a page and read it—"Amanda liked to be on top which was fine with me." The rest was drenched in salad dressing. Something about Amanda's breast . . . or her breath.

My phone rang. I took my purse from around my neck and rummaged inside for the phone. By the time I found it, the phone stopped ringing. Something crawled up my dress. I screamed and tried to shake it off. While flailing around, I dropped the phone.

While searching for the phone, I found a crumpled piece of paper and read it—"I was in love with Amanda, and she was in love with someone who didn't love her as much as me." Kip wasn't much of writer.

My phone rang again. I dug through the garbage, following the sound of the ring. The phone stopped ringing, but I kept digging. I couldn't afford to lose that phone. While I was digging, someone dumped another load of garbage in the dumpster.

I brushed the garbage off my head and continued to search for the phone. I found another crumpled paper, covered in tomato sauce—"She had the fame, and Mike had the horny . . . honey . . . money." It was hard to read. I was losing the light.

I was dumpster diving in the dark. My phone rang again. I was like a Pavlovian dog pawing through the garbage at the sound of a bell. I had to find it while it was still ringing. I dove deeper. It rang two, three, four times. I found it covered in something that felt like custard at the bottom of the dumpster.

I answered the creamy phone. It was Emma. She said my mother had a heart attack.

11

THE MOTHER LOAD

I was driving to the hospital in heavy traffic, screaming at other cars to get out of my way. Then screaming at my mother. Loving her, hating her, trying to save her. I had made this life-or-death drive ten times in as many years. Each one made me crazier. I wished she would die already. A driver cut me off. "My mother is dying!" Tears were streaming down my face. I was terrified of losing her.

I raced through the hospital lobby and rang for the elevator, pushing the button over and over. I forgot how bad I looked and smelled after the dumpster. I got on the elevator. People retreated to the corners. A little girl hid behind her mother's leg. As I had hidden behind my mother's leg. I could not lose that leg, not yet.

I got to the waiting room outside the ICU. Emma was there with Gary and his brother, Ronald, the renowned cardiologist and asshole. No one recognized me in my garbage-strewn disguise.

"How is she?" I cried.

"How is who?" Ronald asked the malodorous stranger.

"My mother!"

"Billie?" Gary gasped.

"Oh, my God," my anguished daughter said.

Ronald snickered. "June is doing better than you. She went into

A-fib and had a mild infarction. We think it was due to an overdose of her thyroid medication. She's stabilized now, they're moving her to a room. It was a self-induced crisis."

A brunette sauntered over to Gary with a cup of coffee. "Here you go, honey."

"You brought a date to my mother's emergency?!" I yelled at Gary.

"We were on our way to dinner when I got a call from Emma saying she couldn't reach you."

"You know this woman?" the brunette asked Gary.

"She's my ex-wife."

"Your ex-wife is homeless?"

"She not homeless, she's nuts."

Emma peeled a strand of spaghetti from my head. "Why is there spaghetti in your wig?"

"I was in a dumpster."

"You let the mother of your child go hungry?" the brunette asked Gary.

"She's not hungry, she's nuts."

"I'm not nuts, I'm a dick," I insisted.

Emma picked more spaghetti from my wig. "What were you doing in a dumpster?"

"I was looking for clues in a murder case."

"Why would you need in a wig in a dumpster?" Ronald snickered.

"It started as a stakeout, the suspect knew what I looked like so I needed a disguise."

"*Stakeout. Suspect.* Do you hear yourself?" Gary chided.

"Do you *smell* yourself?" Emma added.

It kills me when Emma sides with Gary. So I pulled a June and made her feel guilty. "He can't hurt me anymore, but you can tear my heart out."

I left them in my dust—a tiny trail of dirt from the dumpster— and walked off to see my mother. When I got to the ICU, Watson was beside the bed, watching over June. I don't know a better definition of friendship. Watson hugged me, garbage and all. "Are you okay?" I was okay because someone thought to ask.

My mother woke up. The monitors beeped as she berated me. "Nice of you to stop by. Luckily, I'm still alive." She had her face on—eyeliner and rouge were in place. But the dead cat of curls on top of her head was askew. It's funny what makes you love someone. I burst into tears. "That's better," she said.

I explained my appearance. June found the wig disturbing so I took it off. My head was filled with pin curls to anchor the wig. "That's worse," she said. I shook the debris out of the wig and put it back on.

My mother began talking about her near-death experience. Watson interrupted. "It wasn't my fault, Billie, I didn't change her meds."

June confirmed that was true and turned it into a dig at me. "I took some extra thyroid medication. I was so lonely and blue, I needed something to perk me up."

"You wanted to scare the shit out of me," I said.

"That too."

Two orderlies wheeled my mother out of the ICU. Watson and I followed the gurney down the corridor. I brought Watson up to speed on the case and gave her the crumpled pages from the dumpster to clean and file.

As it turned out, Kip had to postpone writing his book. He got a job. He was playing the villain in a western that was shooting in Montana. The red-carpet meltdown had producers seeing him in a new light—as the bad guy. His distorted face was now an asset. Amanda also left town. She said it was to escape the paparazzi, but Margo heard she was having her eyes done. With Kip and Amanda out of the house, there was no point in my going back. But the job turned into a windfall for George. Amanda was having him redo the whole house. He gave me back my credenza as a commission.

I did daily hospital duty with June. Watson wouldn't do. It had to be me. Mostly we watched TV and argued. "You OD'd on thyroid medication. Last time you drank your eyedrops. You're suicidally inept."

June held her fibrillating heart. "I just wanted a little attention."

She flipped around the channels. *TMZ* did a segment on Kip

86

and Amanda. I had to brag. "That's who I'm investigating."

June was fascinated. I relished the attention—that need goes both ways. My mother is very taken with celebrities. She desperately wanted to be one, failing that, she wanted me to be one. My case was as close as I got.

Emma arrived with flowers. "Hello, I must be going."

"Hello, *I* must be going," I said. Emma was supposed to relieve me.

"Hello, then go!" June told us both.

"I have to get back to work," Emma said.

"And I have to get back to my case," I told my daughter.

June interjected, "Billie's case is very interesting. Amanda Baron and that husband of hers are two of the suspects."

Emma was impressed. "Seriously?"

"That's why I was digging in the dumpster."

"Who hired you?"

"I can't divulge my client. But it has to do with Mike Armstrong's murder."

Emma's eyes widened. All three of us were impressed with fame. When I was a kid, my mother read movie magazines. When Emma was a kid, her mother watched televised versions like *Entertainment Tonight*. Caring which movie star is screwing whom is an inherited trait.

I told my enthralled mother and daughter about the famous players in my case. It was the longest I had ever sustained their attention. I told them about Franky McVery's party, implying I was invited. Working out with Gunther and Kip. Helping Amanda select her dress. Being on the red carpet during the slug fest.

Emma forgot "she must be going." But her boss called, and she had to leave. She started out, then turned to say good-bye. "My mother the dick."

June started to get sleepy. She fought to stay awake. Her head would dip and come back up. "I'm afraid to go to sleep. I'm afraid you won't be here when I wake up."

"I'll be here."

"I'm afraid I won't wake up at all. I don't want to go on tour." Her head dipped a few more times and she fell asleep. With her lids closed, I could see how uneven the eyeliner was. The pink circles of unblended rouge, the pancake makeup settled into the wrinkles. I thought about her looking in the mirror and slapping paint over the fear. I loved that courageous, ridiculous face.

I got so upset about the prospect of losing her, I had to walk it off. I went up and down the hospital corridors, dissipating my cortisol. I walked past the vending machines. Candy had not passed my lips since my session with Olga. I was like an addict, staring at the Butterfinger behind the glass. Screw immortality! Quarters flew from my sweaty hand into the machine. I took one hit of chocolate, and the flood gates opened. I was on my third packet of Oreos when I ran out of change. I went running down the halls. "Who can break a ten-dollar bill?" When I was full, I staggered back to June's room and slept off my relapse.

June got better, as she always does. But I was a basket case. So I went to see Krasny. I made myself very hard to help. I was late for my appointment and belligerent. "I don't think this is working. I can't sleep, I'm eating crap, I'm not making any progress on my case, I'm fat, I'm old, and it's your fault."

"How's your mother?"

"Back from the dead and giving me grief."

"That's why you're self-destructing. You're guilty about her suffering, so you're hurting yourself."

"You think?" His comment was so obvious I found it insulting. "I want a refund." He let me percolate and then I blew. "I can't stand to be around her, and I can't bear to lose her. When she does go, it may be at my hand. Then I'll throw myself on her grave and go with her."

"Relationships are complicated, there is a lot of anger and a lot of love, especially with a parent. We feel *both*. Because we love, we have guilt about the anger. They're just feelings. Everybody has them. I imagine your mother does too."

"Her mother was a nightmare. She'd dress June up like Shirley Temple and make her sing and dance. She could tap dance before she could walk." I felt bad for my mother. The dead cat of curls on top of her head was her imitation of Shirley.

"You give both, you get both," I found myself saying. "When I was a kid, June took me swimming at the St. George Hotel in Brooklyn. I bellyflopped into the deep end. I was going under for the third time when she jumped in the pool with her clothes on. Her dress billowed around her as she carried me to safety. As soon as she knew I was okay, she started yelling at me. She saved me and made me feel like shit. My mother is a master of *both*."

Krasny shrugged, he could speak volumes with his shoulders. I left his office at peace with my ambivalence. There would be no refund.

June was back home. Her little infarction was good for our relationship. I was more attentive and so was she. She always asked about my case, which was stalled at the moment, I had lost momentum. Now that June was invested in my career, I had a new impetus to succeed.

When the handyman came to install a safety bar for her to grip in the shower, she introduced me as "My daughter the dick."

The handyman misunderstood and came to my defense. "I'm sure your daughter means well." Her daughter was smiling and so was June.

12

FLOOD SONG

I bellyflopped into Amanda's pool. I was drowning. Amanda ran out of the house in the Valentino dress she wore on the red carpet and dove into the pool. Instead of saving me, she started splashing water in my face. "I trusted you with my behind, and you accuse me of murder!" Splash, splash, splash.

When I woke up from my strange dream, the bed was sopping wet. It was raining inside the loft. Water fell from cracks in the ceiling. I jumped out of bed and was standing in six inches of water. Everything was drenched, even the murder board was wet. I pried my door open and waded into the hallway.

I pounded on Hacker's door, waking him up. He rubbed his eyes. "Talk about a wet dream." Water dripped on his spiked hair and trickled down to his smile. Hacker was young and life was an odyssey, the odder the better.

There are three floors in the building. The third floor was unoccupied. The owner used it for storage. He was the old guy who manufactured men's hats. His slumlord son only showed up if the rent was late. The water was coming from the third floor. It leaked down to the second floor, which leaked to the first floor.

Ivan the Outraged carried his paintings outside to protect them. "I have a show in four days!" Candy's nightgown was wet and transparent. Hacker was in heaven—geeks have a thing for goddesses. Candy was nude in Ivan's paintings, so flaunting her assets was no big deal.

Harpo was bailing water out of his loft. He had some musicians coming over and couldn't ask them to play their electric guitars while standing in water. No one knew what to do. Then Watson arrived and saved the day. She called her former employer, the plumber. Eddie and his sump pump were on the way.

I went to my loft to put on some clothes. Logan appeared at my stenciled door. He sloshed inside. "Billie Ridley Underwater Detective."

I tried to hide how happy I was to see him. "Don't you ever call first?"

"It's one of the perks of being a cop. I just show up, and you have to talk to me."

I started bailing water. "I'm a little busy right now."

Logan grabbed a bucket and bailed. "I had Kip and Amanda under surveillance. My guys saw you at the house, so don't deny it."

"My friend, George, is their interior designer. I needed a job, so he hired me to assist him. It was all perfectly legal. No license required."

"So what did you find out?"

"Amanda prefers ecru to eggshell."

Logan stopped bailing. "I'll show you mine, if you show me yours."

I went first. "I heard Kip say he was *lying* for Amanda. I'm not sure what the lie was, but Amanda freaked out."

"Kip was her alibi. He said they went to bed early the night Mike was killed."

"If they were in bed, it wasn't together. Kip sleeps in the maid's room."

"I know. He said so on the red carpet, knowing the cops would see that interview. Maybe he's setting Amanda up. Kill her lover and have her take the rap."

I told him about Kip's threat to write a tell-all book. "Why write a book implicating himself?" It didn't make sense.

We waded over to the murder board, which was covered in Saran Wrap to keep it dry. Logan wanted to know why I suspected Whitey. I told him about the off-shore deals with Mike. Logan was impressed. "How could you possibly know about that?"

"You don't want to know. You'd have to arrest me."

Watson walked in with the plumber. "What's the Po-Po doing here?"

"Hello, Watson," Logan said.

"How do I get into the unit above you?" the plumber asked.

"Nobody lives there," I told him. "And we can't reach the landlord."

"Maybe I can help," Logan said. We walked up the waterfall on the stairs and got to the third floor. Logan told us to stand back, then he charged the door and broke in. "The Po-Po are always glad to be of service."

I thanked him profusely and so did the plumber. Logan got a call and had to go back to the station. I watched him from the window, he was rubbing his door-busting shoulder as he walked to his car. Nothing gets to me like a man walking away. Especially a man who breaks down doors for me. I made myself look away, that broad shoulder was married.

The pipe was so corroded it burst at the joint. Eddie, the plumber, turned off the water and went to work. He was black, with graying hair and eyes as warm as Watson's. She was assisting him. The woman knew her way with a wrench.

My curious neighbors gathered in the uninhabited loft to look around. No one had ever been inside. Hacker said he sometimes heard strange noises. Candy thought it was haunted. Max Spiegel owned the building. There was still a sign outside that said, "Spiegel Hats." Max was living in a retirement home. His son, Lenny, was waiting for the old man to die so he could sell.

When Max stopped making hats he stored all the antiquated equipment in the loft. It looked like it hadn't been touched in forty years. Dusty sewing machines, spinners that turned spools of wool into felt cones, blockers to shape the cones into hats. And fifty wooden heads wearing all kinds of hats. Fedoras, bowlers, pork pies, derbies, homburgs, panamas. It was a magical trip into a fashionable past.

All of us were putting on hats, even Eddie, who went with the newsboy cap of his youth. I chose a fedora that reminded me of Bogart. Best of all was Harpo in a top hat. He still wears it in tribute to his namesake. The lofts were all flooded, so we hung out in the halls and sat on the stoop, wearing our hats. I got to know my neighbors much better.

Harpo was recording a song that would be used in a movie. This was his big break, and he was running out of time. Musicians were starting to show up, and water was still leaking into his loft. But Harpo never lost his cool. He didn't need to walk off his anxiety, he sang it away, strummed away his stress, his foot always tapping to some inner beat. He lives and breathes music. It's good to be Harpo.

Ivan was not so cool. He was having a show on the weekend. His loft doubled as a gallery. It was a group show because he couldn't get enough buyers to attend on his own. I got one of my better ideas. I asked him to add another artist—Danny. I'd get Margo involved and we'd pack the place with Mike's friends. I could get the suspects in one place and see what happens. I called Sarah, who was very grateful. It was a win for everyone, even Ivan.

Eddie was still pumping water out of the building. I sat on the stoop with Watson and Candy, a very unlikely trio of women. Candy is from Alabama. Her breathy Monroe is combined with a Southern accent. I could listen to her talk all day. "Marilyn slept in a bra to keep her breasts firm. People say they stuck straight out. She used Vaseline on her skin. It gave her those little white hairs. I have them too." Candy showed us the faint white hairs on her face.

"Before she was famous, Marilyn had a list of men she wanted to sleep with—John Huston, Elia Kazan, Charles Laughton, Arthur Miller, Albert Einstein. She got Miller and some say, Einstein. Kennedy wasn't even on the list. The dress she wore to sing "Happy Birthday Mr. President" sold for a million dollars. The white dress from *Seven Year Itch* sold for five million. I have one just like it. Sometimes I wear it and stand over a fan, when I want to get my Marilyn on."

Watson had her own list of potential lovers. "Kanye. Denzel.

Michael Jordan."

"No white guys?" I asked.

"George Clooney. If I absolutely had to."

Candy's list also included Clooney. Along with Johnny Depp, Stephen Soderbergh, Tarantino, Damon and Affleck, either Coen Brother, Ryan Gosling, David Fincher . . . " and so on and so on, it was a long list.

I admired Marilyn's list and given my advanced age, I included the dead. "Einstein. Miller. Spencer Tracy. And Clooney, if I absolutely had to include the living."

It took Eddie ten hours to pump out the water. As a favor to Watson, he only charged five hundred bucks. I saw Watson hug Eddie before he left. She watched him drive off until his truck was long out of sight. I was curious but cautious, she was that tender. I waited until we were alone.

"So you and Eddie, what's the deal?"

Answering me was an act of trust. "He's my father."

I liked Eddie and didn't understand the problem. "And?"

"He didn't know about me till thirty-three years after I came along. Momma was dying and didn't want me to be alone, so she told him he had a daughter. Eddie was married when they hooked up, he still is. It's a secret he's my daddy. You're the only one I told." Watson and I got a lot closer that day. Floods can be blessings in disguise.

And the blessings kept coming. I was lying in bed, studying the murder board. There was a rhythmic tapping on my door. Harpo needed a favor. His backup singer got another gig and never showed up. He wanted me to come downstairs and sing backup.

"Me?" I gushed.

"I've heard you singing my stuff in the shower."

"Really?"

"Let's do it, dude."

Ten minutes later I was in Harpo's loft, standing in front of a microphone. The band wasn't so sure about the old lady who lived upstairs. The guys on guitar and bass were both named Jerry. The drummer was Dog. When I walked in, Dog gave me a rimshot, thinking it was a gag. Hacker, the all-purpose techie, was the engineer. He stood in a converted closet that housed a console and mixing board. Hacker gave me two thumbs up from behind the glass wall.

The song was called "Dancin' To My Own Tune." I heard them rehearsing and already knew it. It was an in-your-face anthem for anyone rebelling against anything, and it was impossible not to dance to. Harpo had a hit. And I would be a tiny giddy grateful part of it.

Harpo told me he wanted Merry Clayton on the Rolling Stone's "Gimme Shelter." A soulful high-octave echo of his lead vocal. "You're a little white, but that's alright."

He taught me my part and we tried a take. I was rocking and wailing. The band was blown away, literally. I was so loud, I blew an amp. I could only hit the high notes at full volume. But I brought a good energy to the room. The Jerrys said they had to play from their nuts just to keep up.

We took a break, and I told the guys about being a K-Girl—the Fly Girls of my generation. Murray the K was a DJ in New York who did local TV shows with The Byrds, The Who, all the greats. We taped a show at Shea Stadium and James Brown walked around the bases singing "It's a Man's World" to the K-Girls. I was on third base.

That was my best rock 'n' roll story. Until that night at Harpo's.

We did a few more takes and then we nailed it. The ultimate meeting of moments. The one you take to your grave. We rocked the building and touched the sky. These were my brothers, or sons, or whatever. I'm old, but I'm cool. I'm with the band.

13
MIXED SIGNALS

The next day I was still rocking. I sang in the shower, danced myself dressed. Watson took June to physical therapy. Her doctor said she needed to move more. I gave her a copy of Gunther's DVD so we could move together. Come dumpster or high water, I moved with Gunther. My thighs were firmer, my gut didn't obstruct my view of the scale. I renewed my vow of immortality and had a green drink.

Sarah and Danny were on their way over. He was taking his paintings to Ivan's gallery. My occupation was stenciled on the door, there was no point in trying to hide it. Maybe I'd achieve more if my investigation was in the open. But I covered the murder board and turned it toward the wall. It's impolite to let your guests know they're suspects.

When they arrived, Billie Ridley Private Detective explained herself. I told them partial truths about investigating Mike and sidestepped the rest, enough to calm Danny and regain Sarah's trust. She thought it was brave to become a detective at my age. I hustled them off to Ivan's. I liked Sarah and wanted to keep the lies to a minimum.

I was a big fan of Danny's work. Tortured as he was, hostile, rude, erratic, he was incredibly talented. Actually, that describes most of the painters the world pays millions of dollars to own.

Ivan was thrilled with the impressive RSVPs. Margo got everyone to attend by promising them bad press if they declined. How could they abandon the son of their dear friend who died so tragically? The implication being that perhaps they had a reason to stay away—like maybe they killed him.

When we walked in, Ivan gave Danny a bear hug and a booming, "Welcome."

Danny stood stiffly. "Hello."

Ivan showed us around the gallery, which had finally dried out. Ivan's paintings were mostly self-portraits and nudes of his various muses. Sarah was gracious, straining to find nice things to say. Danny was underwhelmed by Ivan's work. Until he saw a nude of Candy and was stopped in his tracks. "Magnificent," he murmured. It was in response to the blonde, not the artist.

"My platinum period," Ivan said. "Let's take a look at your work." He helped Danny get his paintings from Sarah's Land Rover. It was a stunning collection. I felt sorry for Ivan. You could see it on his face, the envy, the remorse. Danny was gifted and would go the distance.

They started hanging Danny's paintings. Front and center was a portrait of Mike that he had just done. Danny had conveyed him so movingly. Sarah saw my intense reaction. But I covered pretty well. "Mike was a dead ringer for my dad."

Candy came home wearing shorts and a tank top. She explained her unseasonal attire in her breathy Monroe. "I just came from an audition. They wanted Daisy Duke with an edge." Danny was in deep lust. Ivan asserted his sexual superiority over the superior artist by kissing an adoring Candy. Goddesses go for womanizers.

Danny insisted his mother and I make ourselves scarce while he hung paintings and coveted Candy. When we got upstairs, Sarah apologized for her son. "Danny has his father's penchant for beautiful women. Without the skill to close."

I decided to tell Sarah who my client was. Felicia was my employer, but she was also a suspect, as was her father. Sarah probably had a good take on both of them. "Felicia hired me to find out if Mike was having an affair."

Sarah couldn't contain her glee. "I don't wish anyone that kind of pain. But he was *my* adulterous husband before she took him away." She opened up about Felicia, who was also Danny's step-mother. He spent every other weekend in Felicia's picture-perfect home. Sarah had been civil for Danny's sake.

"Felicia was nice to Danny, but kept her distance. She was too nice to me. Her compassion for poor Sarah was to remind me she won. Or maybe I just saw it that way, because poor Sarah was still in love with Mike." She said more than she intended and tried to bury it. "Other than her being rich and beautiful, I never understood the attraction." I smiled and she went on. "She's so cold and calculating, it had to be like sleeping with a stone."

"Sometimes thighs can be too firm."

"The real attraction was Oliver Whitney's prestige. I couldn't compete with that."

I wanted to know more about Whitey. "I understand they didn't get along."

"It was typical Mike. He hated Oliver and desperately wanted to be him. Big international deals were a long way from running numbers in the Bronx. A lot of money was coming in. Mike became very secretive. I thought they were doing something illegal. But the secrecy was because he was leaving me for Oliver's daughter."

Sarah was a suspect, but she was also a friend. I stopped pumping her and we just hung out. We talked about kids, parents, varicose veins. But she always returned to the subject of Mike. "He lived and loved with everything he had, then he moved on and loved someone else." I was grateful Gary was unremarkable. Him you could get over.

Danny hung his paintings. He was ready to go. Sarah and I hugged good-bye. If I was nice to Sarah, I was okay with him. "Thanks for the gallery."

I tried to draw him out. "You're really good, Danny. Mike would have been very proud."

"He would have been prouder if I was boning Candy." Weird as he was, I liked this kid. As they were leaving, he high-fived me. "Later, Billie."

"Later."

I rolled out the murder board and stuck a dollar bill next to Whitey. Maybe Mike wasn't killed for love, he was killed for money. Hacker hacked into their offshore accounts. There were several withdrawals right before Mike's death. The money motive had potential.

I compensated Hacker with a healthy meal—kale and cannellini beans. Beans are an Olga must, but rinse off the syrup to avoid gas. It's a simple recipe. Heat some olive oil and add a little Health Valley Chicken Broth, which has six grams of protein per cup. Saute onions, garlic, and the beans until tender. Add the kale until it wilts and turns a brilliant green.

Watson joined us for lunch. She wouldn't touch a green drink, but she loved this. I had an epiphany—healthy can taste good. It was the start of my culinary quest for *both*.

Hacker scarfed his down and asked for more. God knows he needed it. He was so pale. He rarely went out. Even in the flood, he never ventured further than the stoop.

"What's so great about outside?" he asked.

"The sky," I replied.

"Pollution, the hole in the ozone, skin cancer, acid rain."

"People."

"Diseases, muggings, getting dumped by some girl I haven't met yet."

My door buzzed. "That may be her." I looked through the frosted glass and opened the door. "Danny." I was surprised to see him again.

He was annoyed at my surprise. "I said *later*. It's later."

"How did you get here?"

"The bus," he said, as he followed me inside.

"These are my friends, Watson and Hacker."

Danny ignored them and headed for the murder board. "What's this?"

"It's just a way for me to organize my thoughts."

Danny poked his picture. "Am I a suspect?"

I didn't know what to say, so I gambled on the truth. "Everybody is."

He looked at the picture of Sarah. "My mother is a suspect?"

"Who doesn't want to kill their ex?" Watson said.

Danny poked at pictures and asked about the other suspects. I deflected his questions and offered him something to eat. "You think I killed my father and you're inviting me to lunch?"

Watson dished him up a plate. Hacker pulled out a barstool and Danny sat down. "Thank you . . . Hacker." Danny eyed him suspiciously. "Is that your real name?"

"What I do is who I am."

"I'm Painter." They seemed to get along, speaking in geek and eating their kale. "I have Asperger's," Danny announced. Any potential friend needed to know up front.

Hacker tried to put him at ease. "A lot of cool guys had Asperger's—Einstein, Picasso."

Danny listed the afflicted at lightning speed. "Beethoven Darwin Edison Hitchcock Jefferson Kandinsky Mozart Nietzsche Newton Shaw Van Gogh Warhol."

"That's some club," Hacker said.

"Yeah." Danny avoided eye contact. I couldn't tell if he was pleased or upset. This kid was so hard to read. After some awkward conversation about art, cars, kale, Danny said he was going home. It would take forever on the bus, so I offered him a lift.

We got in my Civic and headed for Beverly Hills. From the moment we buckled up, Danny said he wanted to drive. It was a loop that repeated every mile. "I have a learner's permit. I drive all the time. I need to practice before my test." The closer we got to our destination, the more intense the request. We were approaching La Brea when Danny offered me a bribe. "If you let me drive, I'll tell you a secret about my dad." He had me and he knew it. "Pull over."

I pulled over and we switched seats. He started the engine and took off. I asked him the secret. He lowered the windows. "I like the wind in my hair." It made it harder to hear him, but I didn't want to argue while he was at the wheel. He looked over at me. "Are you afraid?"

I peeled my hair out of my eyes. "A little."

"I can never tell how people feel. If they make a smiley face, I know they're happy. If they cry, I know they're sad. Anything else I don't get." No wonder he was so hard to read. Feelings were a mystery, even his own.

We came to a stoplight, and he told me the secret. "The day before he died, my dad told me he was going to be a father again. Felicia is pregnant."

I didn't want him to know I already knew. "That's very interesting."

The light changed and he hit the gas. "I slept over at his house. Felicia didn't feel well so she went to bed. Me and my dad had dinner alone. That's when he told me."

"Does your mother know about the baby?"

"I don't want to talk about my mom." He started to drive more recklessly.

"Now I'm afraid." I put my hands on my cheeks like the kid in *Home Alone*—"This is fear."

"I thought that was surprise."

We almost hit a parked car. "You can tell by the tone of my voice. *Slow down!*"

"Is that fear or anger?"

"Pull over!"

"It sounds like anger." He picked up speed. I was no longer angry, I was terrified.

He ignored a traffic signal and raced through an intersection. "RED LIGHT!" I shrieked.

Danny seemed amused. Every time we stopped, he would slam on the brakes and yell, "RED LIGHT!" I don't know why, but a few stops later, I started to laugh. All the way home, at every single stop, we'd both scream, "RED LIGHT!" Was that anger, fear, hysteria? I no longer knew how I felt, I was as lost as Danny.

I still think about that death-defying ride. It was a harbinger of things to come.

14
ART AND SEX

Margo was expecting a stellar turnout for the gallery opening. Ivan dumped the other artists so it would be just him and Danny. Mike's son would have an A-list debut. And I would have my suspects under one roof.

Kip and Amanda were both attending. The public fighting had been great for their careers. She got financing for her movie. He got cast as the villain in a Batman movie. So they stayed together and squabbled for the cameras, keeping fame alive.

I told Felicia the gallery was a device to get the people in Mike's life together and see how they interact. I was trying to entice her and it worked. She said she was coming to support Danny. I wanted Felicia in the mix. She was my employer, but she was also a suspect.

I stood in Stella's closet, trying on clothes. I was going to the opening as myself. I wasn't sure who that was or what she would wear. I decided on a tasteful skirt and blouse. Attractive but appropriate for my age and occupation. I guess. I poured hot water in my tight high heels, then I put them on and walked around in search of myself.

Ivan's little gallery was wall-to-wall star-studded Friends of Mike. The cognoscenti of the LA art world were also in attendance.

They were duly impressed with Danny. Ivan was old news and pretty much ignored.

Margo arrived with George and Limber as her dates. The trio had become a celebrated example to anyone still in the closet. George, the interior designer and dictator of taste, flipped over Danny's work and bought two paintings for his clients. Everyone had to have an original Danny Armstrong. Prices were discreetly doubled.

Danny was agitated by all the attention. And by Candy. She wore a knockoff of Marilyn's iconic white dress. Ivan was with a former muse, flirting in full view of Candy. His womanizing ways lost their appeal. Candy broke up with him in a breathy tirade and left with her edgy Daisy Duke director.

Franky McVery made a drunk and disorderly rock star entrance. The crowd parted as he crossed the room. I followed in his wake as he headed for the bar. He saw Sarah and stopped to kiss her hand. The words tumbled out in his charming Irish rasp. "Mike was a fool for losing you."

Sarah did not disagree. They talked about old times. Then she introduced me. "This is my friend, Billie." Everyone was looking our way, and I wanted to matter.

"*Hullabaloo*," I blurted out.

Franky turned to me and tried to focus. "Beg pardon?"

"It was eons ago but we have a history. I danced in a cage while you sang."

Franky came to attention. "I always fancied those luscious little dancers."

I did an arm-flailing Watusi. "It's never too late."

Franky danced along, then he leaned me back and kissed me. People were appalled. How could he kiss a woman his age? My team cheered us on. Hacker and Harpo applauded. Watson pimped me out. "She lives upstairs if you want another taste."

"She's a private detective," Danny warned.

Franky retreated. "I'd better behave myself." He put an arm around Danny. "Show Uncle Franky some art, lad." Was it my profession that scared him off? Kiss or no kiss, Franky remained a suspect.

Norman Kaufman had flown in from his Vegas location. He hid in a corner, staring at a painting of a man jumping off a cliff. I went over to casually pump him, but a Studio Suit beat me to the punch. "I hear you're having some problems."

The veins in Norman's scrawny neck popped out. "An actor finds God and wants the hit man he's playing to be redeemed, so I have him save a kid. He loses God when his girlfriend screws an extra, so we reshoot the redemption and kill the kid. But the kid has hepatitis and gives it to the actor, so we have to recast. Which part of that Kafkaesque saga is the director's fault?"

Norman bought the painting and went back to Vegas. It was a quick round-trip. He often blew in and out of town for casting sessions and was back at work by morning. I didn't know the motive, but Norman had ample time to kill Mike.

Felicia made a tentative entrance. She accepted condolences and declined invitations from Mike's friends. I stayed by her side. When she saw Danny and Sarah, she surprised me by gripping my hand. Under that polished exterior was desperation. "Don't leave me alone."

Sarah was thrown by my holding Felicia's hand. Danny's agitation was palpable. Felicia admired his paintings. Danny kept his eyes on her belly. "You're going to have a baby."

Felicia squeezed my hand. "That's right, Danny."

"Congratulations," Sarah said evenly.

Danny's stare grew more intense. "Is it a girl or a boy?"

Felicia dropped my hand to protect her belly. "It's a boy."

Sarah rose to the occasion and soothed her son. "You're going to have a little brother."

"Half brother," Danny replied.

Sarah soothed some more. "He will be family. A part of your father. It's okay with me if you're happy about it."

"I don't know what I am. I never do."

Kip and Amanda arrived and immediately went their separate ways, with Kip heading for the bar. Amanda was ravishing, the glam squad outdid themselves. Margo said Amanda had blepharoplasty—all traces of mourning Mike had been surgically removed from under her eyes.

Felicia and Sarah were united in their resentment of a mutual rival. I dissed Amanda in allegiance to my client. "That's not her ass, she puts pads in her Spanx."

Mike's two wives smiled. But Danny was upset. "How do you know that?"

"I worked for Amanda, posing as her decorator's assistant." I comforted the jealous wives with another dis. "That's not her hair, Amanda wears extensions."

Sarah said bitterly, "One wonders what Mike was so drawn to."

We were about to find out. Amanda swept across the room and headed our way. It was such a complicated dynamic, all three women had reason to resent each other. Mike was sleeping with Amanda, but he never married her. He was married to Sarah for nineteen years. But he left her for Felicia. Felicia was paying me to find out why he was sleeping with Amanda . . . and Pam and Jessica and God knows who else. He left a lot of broken hearts behind. He even made a dent in mine.

Amanda embraced Danny. "You're so talented."

Danny stood stiffly. "Hello."

Amanda said polite things to Mike's wives. Sarah and Felicia were civil, mostly for Danny's sake. He was starting to twitch.

Amanda's violet eyes met mine. "What are you doing here?"

"She's a private detective," Danny announced.

A million emotions crossed Amanda's face. She settled on surprise." And a very good actress. I had no idea." Kip joined us with a drink in either hand.

"You remember Billie," Amanda said.

Kip took a disinterested look, then he placed me. "George's assistant."

"She's a private detective," Danny twitched.

Kip glared at me. "Well, aren't you the lying little bitch?"

Amanda flashed a false smile. "Not all of his insults are reserved for me."

The air was already thick with intrigue, then Pam joined the mix. Felicia clutched my hand. Pam said her hellos. She looked at me curiously. "Billie?"

I beat Danny to the punch—"I'm a private detective. That's why

I was at Mike's office."

Pam upped her status as a suspect by having no reaction. "It's nice to see you again." Her eyes landed on Felicia's hand clutching mine. You could see her try to calculate what that meant.

Ivan swaggered over, drawn by Amanda's celebrity. "I'm so glad you could come." Amanda batted her augmented lashes. "I'd love to paint you sometime."

"What else would you like to do to my wife?" Kip asked Ivan.

Ivan backed off. "I just want to paint her."

"You're not good enough. If you wanted to fuck her, that's another story."

Amanda told Kip, "There are no cameras, darling, don't waste your venom."

Pam slid away to look at Danny's paintings. She went right to the portrait of Mike. She stared at it, transfixed. He was wearing his *All My Love* watch. Pam wanted to buy the painting. The price was ten grand, more than an assistant would normally spend. She was willing to expose her feelings for Mike, she wanted it that badly.

Ivan's dealer, a pretentious old-timer, was representing Danny. Amanda was also interested in the painting. The dealer was mesmerized by the movie star. Amanda raised the stakes and outbid Pam. "I'll give you twenty thousand."

Two women fighting over her husband made Felicia mad. "I'll give you thirty."

The dealer was thrilled. "Thank you, Mrs. Armstrong."

"That isn't fair." Pam's protest was ignored by the widow and the mistress. Amanda upped the ante again. "Forty thousand."

Kip was being cuckolded by a canvas. "You bring that thing home and I'll piss all over it."

The impromptu auction was drawing a crowd. Amanda was not about to back down. "Forty-five thousand."

Kip hissed at Amanda, "You're bidding against yourself!"

Felicia stood her ground. "Fifty thousand."

Amanda countered. "Sixty!"

"Seventy!" Felicia said indignantly. "I was his *wife*."

Danny got between them. "The painting is not for sale!" That shut everybody up. He took the painting off the wall and gave it to Sarah. "This belongs to you." Every first wife in the room, including this one, was cheering inside.

By the end of the evening, all of Danny's paintings had sold. Ivan the Also Ran only sold the two nudes of Candy—one to Hacker and one to Danny.

The show was over, the Friends of Mike were starting to leave. I noticed a steely-eyed tough guy lingering behind. He looked familiar, but I couldn't place him. I took his picture with the hidden camera embedded in my purse. He seemed to know what I was doing and faced away. He headed for the exit. I plowed through the crowd and followed him outside.

The paparazzi were snapping celebs as they waited for the valet to bring their cars. Kip and Amanda were doing an encore. "I'm not getting in a car with you," Amanda declared as their Bentley pulled up.

"I could tie you to the hood with your extensions."

I looked up and down the street, the tough guy had disappeared. I ran around the corner. He was driving off in a black Lexus! He was too far away to get the plates, but I knew this was the guy who'd been following me. Lexus was no phantom.

Watson and I went upstairs. I told her about Lexus, and we discussed who he might be. He remained a mystery, but at least he had a face. I made copious notes on the murder board about all the suspects that were at the gallery. It had been a long night. We were both wiped out, so I sent Watson home.

I was fighting the urge to eat the goodies the caterer left behind. I stood in front of my open fridge, nibbling on carrot sticks, followed by a bite of cheesecake. My battle between thin and temptation was interrupted by my door buzzer.

I looked through the frosted glass. Be still my heart and nether regions. It was Franky McVery. I opened the door. He was falling down drunk and fell on me. "I came back for more." We loped as one to my couch. His legendary tongue was in my mouth. He was delicious, I think it was Kahlua.

Franky saw the murder board and stopped groping. "Is that my picture in your rogue's gallery?" Maybe he was here to pump me about my case, the sexual overture was a just ploy. He groped me again. When a woman is desperate, a ploy is enough.

"It's just a way to help me organize my thoughts," I moaned.

He unbuttoned my blouse. "Am I really a suspect?"

"I suspect everyone," I said as he unhooked my bra.

"But why me?" he asked as he lifted my skirt.

"I was at your party the night Mike was killed . . . " It was hard to talk with his tongue in my mouth.

His hands were all over me. "Then you know I have an alibi."

"You were an hour late," I panted.

"I wanted to piss off my girlfriend so she'd move out." He picked me up and carried me to the bed. Franky dropped his pants and there it was. A rock star erection.

I took it as a compliment. "Thank you."

"It's my Irish blood, I can never get enough." And then he took me. Old as I was. He was expert and tender at the same time. I discovered nerve endings I never knew I had. I was excited, but conflicted. What if he was a murderer? The body wants what the conscience can't handle, and so I gave in. As Big Os go, it was a personal best. All three of them, in ascending order of abandon. When it was over, we both passed out. Beep beep, blink blink. I dreamt I had a lover.

When I woke up he was still there. "Good morning," I blushed.

Franky was hung over. It took him a moment to remember where he was. He squinted at me. "*Hullabaloo.*"

I was nervous and didn't know what happens next. "Are you hungry?"

He kissed my thigh. "Insatiable. But I have to take my little tyke to soccer."

I hid my disappointment. "How many kids do you have?"

"Five. One for each wife. Spawning assures them an income. Did you not see the dollar sign on my ass?"

"They keep you young."

"They keep me touring. My extended brood costs millions to maintain."

My door buzzed. It wasn't Watson, she had a key. More angry buzzing, then pounding. "Sorry," I said to Franky. "I'll be right back." I grabbed a sheet and padded to the door. I peered through the frosted glass. It was wrong of me to be happy, but I couldn't help myself. I had sex with Franky McVery, and Gary was about to find out.

I opened the door very wide, making sure he'd come inside. He walked in complaining. "I've been calling you all night, we're due at the lawyer's office in an hour."

"I must have had my phone turned off."

Gary saw Franky. It was like he'd seen the sun explode. Astonishment, doubt, a blinding light. He closed his eyes and opened them again, but the naked rock star was still in my bed.

I pointed to Franky—"*He* can fuck a sixty-seven-year-old woman."

"Hello," Franky said. Gary just stared at him.

I relished introducing them. "Franky . . . this is Gary, my ex."

Franky got the gist of my joy and played it up. "One man's loss is another man's delight. No hard feelings, mate."

Gary was dumbstruck. But I was looking past him. Logan was standing in the doorway. He froze, assessing the situation. "Maybe I should come back later."

I hiked up my sheet. "That's okay."

Logan walked inside and said angrily, "Why didn't you tell me about the gallery? My guys said all the suspects were there." He looked at the suspect in my bed.

"Hello," Franky said.

Logan looked at Gary. "Who's he?"

"I'm her husband," Gary said.

"*Ex*-husband," I clarified.

"Who are you?" Gary demanded.

"Detective Ruddy Logan, LAPD."

Franky jumped in, "Excuse me, gents, I got here first. Take a number."

There were *three* men fighting over me. "Why don't I put on some coffee?" But the one I really wanted was the one who left.

"No thanks," Logan said as he walked out.

I ran after him, tripping on my sheet. "Wait!" I followed him down the hall. "Logan," I said to his back as he started down the stairs.

He stopped and turned. "Is that how you investigate a suspect?"

"Franky and I go way back—"

"Next time I'll call first." He turned to go.

"You're jealous."

"I'm pissed off."

I chased after him. "Don't go."

He turned back again. "Your lover and your husband?"

"I was lonely and you were taken." There, I said it. He knew how I felt. A lesser man would have kissed me, as he did in my fantasy. But Logan is a good man. And so he left.

I started up the stairs and saw Gary on the landing. I knew he had heard us, I could see it on his face. He passed me on the stairs and didn't say a word. What was there to say? Our ship had sailed, and sunk.

When I got back to the loft, Franky was dressed and ready to go. "That's very appealing, running after another man. I don't get much competition."

I looked at Franky's picture on the murder board which was right behind him. Here he was, in the flesh, with his hand on my ass. I said good-bye to my amorous suspect. "God, I hope you didn't do it."

I was horny, guilty, overwhelmed. So I made a date with yet another man—Krasny. I walked into his office and announced, "I got laid." I was hoping for a bigger reaction. "It was a multiple-orgasm all-nighter." Krasny remained impassive. "It was *Franky McVery.* How about that?" I'm not sure what I wanted, but I wasn't getting it.

"How are you feeling?"

"Properly fucked. Can't you see the glow?" The glow began to fade. I told him about my three-man morning after. And how alone it left me. "They're all unattainable. I guess that's the attraction." Krasny shrugged and nodded at the same time. He does that when I get something right. I yearned for his approval, so I stuck with that theme.

"Logan is married, I feel guilty for even wanting him. Gary was jealous and that was fun. I still feel something for him, but I could never trust him again. Franky was a one-night stand, but a needy woman can dream of more. And I have a posthumous crush on Mike. You can't get more unattainable than dead."

"You lost your father when you were young, unattainable is familiar. You're stuck in a paradox. If you pursue a man who is unavailable, you'll never get the love you want. If he meets you halfway, that's not familiar and so you lose interest."

"How do I bust out of my paradox?"

"Get to your feelings about your father, the love, the anger, the memories that are attached to him. Then you won't need to resolve them in other relationships."

"Here you are being all kind and wise. And now I have a crush on you."

"You'll get over that when you get over Murray."

I started to cry. "I don't want to get over him. Hurting is how I keep him alive."

"That's what you need to work through. The love you can keep."

He was helping me get over unattainable men, and all I could think about was how to attain him. Krasny was married. I googled him after my first session. His wife's name was Alma. She was also an analyst. I wondered if they ever talked about me. In bed at night, a casual mention of his favorite patient, the one he was secretly in love with. These were my nut-lady thoughts as I held his caring gaze.

Krasny smiled. "Longing isn't crazy, Billie. It's human. Nothing to be ashamed of, just something to understand." He was reading my mind. I felt so exposed. But good. He saw me. Somebody, finally. For two hundred dollars a pop.

I was parked across the street from Krasny's office, extending my forty-five minutes. I was his last appointment. He drove out of the garage. I thought about following him, but I'd have to confess what I'd done at my next session. I didn't want to scare him. I didn't want to scare me. I needed to believe I was getting better.

In my single days, when I was torching for a man, I'd drive by his house and see if he was home, and who he was with. I spent many a Saturday night buzzing houses and crying my eyes out. My sexual reawakening had unleashed more need than I could manage. Old habits were stirred. So I buzzed the men I couldn't have.

I was in Beverly Hills, so I drove past the house that I lived in with Gary. The new owners had cut down the oak tree that graced the front yard. I always felt like that tree was protecting me. Now it was gone and so was I.

I drove into the Hollywood Hills, listening to Franky's greatest hits as I headed for his house. He was a suspect, so my buzzing could double as work. I saw a woman half my age walk past the bedroom window wearing a camisole. I can't wear a camisole, my breasts are too low and my arms are too fat. Men can date camisoles into their sixties, all women get is Medicare. They can still father kids, we run out of eggs and become grandmas. Which leads me to believe, if there's a God, he's a guy.

I looked in the mirror and saw a fool. The fool drove to Norman's house, the last place I had ever seen Mike. It was dark and dead inside. Which is how I felt.

My unconscious was at the wheel, I had no choice but to go where it took me. Imagine my surprise when it took me to the police station. I parked across the street, hoping to catch a glimpse of Logan. The Bad Cop entered the building. I don't think he made me, I was wearing a wig. I couldn't tell if my tour of unavailable men was curing myself or feeding my addiction. Was buzzing just a gateway behavior to stalking? I demanded my unconscious take me home.

15
LICENSE THIS!

I was driving down Sunset when I saw the black Lexus in my rearview mirror. I dodged in and out of traffic, he dodged right along with me. I made a U-turn that was right out of a movie, tires screeching, cars honking. It worked—I lost him. I stopped at an IHOP and had a stack of pancakes to calm myself down. Nothing blows a diet like being tailed.

When I got to my hood, I circled the block and didn't see the Lexus. I parked my car and started up the street. There was a guy behind me. I couldn't see his face. His pace picked up with mine. I ran to the corner and ducked inside the Bada Bang. It was nearly empty, a few drunks and some blue-collar regulars. I sat at the bar and got out my cell phone to call Hacker. The bartender shuffled over. "What'll it be?"

Lexus walked in. As he approached me I screamed, "Help!"

The bartender grabbed a baseball bat. "Sounds like you ain't her type."

"I just want to ask the lady some questions. I'm a private investigator." He shoved his laminated license across the bar. His name was Johnny Doyle. A hard-boiled Bogart in his fifties, short-cropped hair, the lines in his face were not from smiling.

I felt like a wimpy imitation. "I'm a private investigator too."

"You're a rank amateur who keeps getting in my way."

"What do you want, Doyle?"

"We need to talk."

"About what?"

"Mike Armstrong."

If I was being pumped I had to be ready to pump back, and I was too rattled. "Not now, I'm going on a stakeout."

"Like you were staking out Franky's place and the police station? I don't think you grasp the concept."

"Call me tomorrow." I handed him my card, which he rejected.

"I've got your number," he said over his shoulder as he headed for the door.

I ordered a Kahlua and milk and gave the burly bartender a ten-dollar tip for coming to my rescue. He told me his name was Tony, he'd bought the bar when he moved here from Jersey. He was a fanatical fan of *The Sopranos*. Not many customers knew the show like I did. I could even talk episodes. Tony grabbed his bat and walked me home. "After midnight the scumbags come out." He kept his bat drawn until I was safely inside. I liked having some local muscle. Even though I don't drink much, the Bada Bang became a hangout.

Watson arrived early the next morning, and I told her about Doyle. We were trying to figure out who he was working for when the door buzzed. I looked through the frosted glass. It was Doyle. No call, no warning. I was still in my pajamas. I opened the door. He paraphrased the stenciling, "Billie Ridley Girl Detective."

Doyle walked inside and looked around. I knew he would scoff at Watson's name, so I used her first name. "This is my assistant, Cleo."

"Cleo Watson," she said to Doyle. "You got something to say about that?"

"Watson," was all he said. He looked at the murder board, then back at me. "You've been watching too much TV." But he walked over and read it.

"Who's Harley?" That seemed to unnerve him.

"That's privileged information."

"That's bullshit. You don't even know his name. Felicia is

wasting her money."

"What makes you think I'm working for her?"

Doyle ignored me. He was looking at the murder board. "Who's June?"

I hid my embarrassment and got cocky. "I'll give up June if you give up Harley."

Doyle looked at Watson who bit her lip. She was trying not to laugh, but he perceived it as tension. Doyle took the bait. "He's a small-time hustler."

"I need a name."

Doyle finally spit it out. "Joey Pallone." He sneered at my smile. "Now it's your turn."

"June is my mother."

Doyle got in my smirking face. "Joey Pallone is my barber."

I was out-duped and I was furious. "You lied to me."

"Who do you think you're dealing with? I'm a pro. You're an unlicensed joke."

"If I'm such a joke, why have you been following me?"

"Because you were following my client." He said it like I should have known. He said everything that way.

"I follow a lot of people." I had no idea which one it was.

"*Mike*," he said impatiently.

I didn't understand. "Who are you working for now?"

"I have no employer. My client is dead and I want to know who killed him." Doyle paused, he seemed to care about Mike. Then he was back on the attack. "I don't want some delusional Nancy Drew screwing up my investigation."

"I think we're done, Doyle."

He imitated me imitating him. "Stay out of my way, Ridley."

Doyle left. I felt like the amateur I was. Watson saw me withering. "You gonna prove that asshole right, or raise yourself up and solve this case?"

I wasn't sure I had it in me. Then I heard music. Harpo started playing our song. A rebellious rallying cry that pounded at me through the floor. It was a transformational moment. Like when Rocky runs up the stairs to his theme song and raises his arms triumphantly. I hopped around with my fist in the air.

I guess Watson didn't see the movie. "This ain't a good time to lose your mind."

My theme song swelled beneath me. "If that dick can follow me, then this dick can follow him." The only thing on the murder board that got a rise out of Doyle was Harley. He was obviously a key player. I would stay on Doyle's tail until he led me to my unidentified suspect. But first I had to find Doyle.

I cooked Hacker a chicken and had him delve into Doyle—his clients were mostly Hollywood heavyweights. He had a reputation for being loyal and breaking the rules. Doyle had been arrested for running a wiretap on a studio head but got off on a technicality. Evidently, Mike was more than a client, he was paying Doyle's legal bills.

I found a photo of Doyle that ran in the *LA Times* and stuck it on the murder board. I considered him a suspect. Trying to solve a murder that you commit is a great cover. Maybe that's why he wanted me to back off.

I made some notes about the night I saw Harley. He rode his bike into The Velvet Swing parking lot and got inside Mike's Porsche. A few minutes later, Harley took off. I was in the Mustang wearing a Beyonce wig. Doyle was in the Lexus, observing me observing Mike. Why did Doyle follow me? What had I seen? If I knew who Harley was, I might have some answers.

I needed another car to tail Doyle, he'd already seen the Mustang and the Civic. I borrowed Hacker's Chevy Volt. He never used it, he never went anywhere. Who knew which disguises Doyle had seen me wear? I needed something completely different. Everything in Stella's closet was so over-the-top. Then it hit me—I would be a man.

I removed my bra and wrapped an ace bandage around my breasts, flattening them against my chest. I wore a short Halle Berry pixie wig, which I smoothed down so it would look more masculine. Stella didn't own any men's clothing, except for the Brooks Brothers suit he'd worn to his bar mitzvah. I shortened the pants and sleeves, otherwise it was a perfect fit. I looked like a very old little boy.

Doyle worked out of his house, a mile above the Sunset Strip. I kept my distance, assuming he had surveillance. I spotted the Lexus driving down Kings Road and followed him to the gym and then to a liquor store. When it got dark, he drove downtown. He headed for my place. I was following someone who was looking for me. He drove by my building and looked in my window. Guess what, Doyle, I'm not there.

He took off. I feared he had spotted the odd little man in the Chevy Volt. He drove through a McDonald's and got some takeout. I followed him to Laurel Canyon. He headed up Wonderland Avenue and turned off his headlights as he drove the last hundred feet. I killed my lights when he killed his. I watched him waiting and watching for three hours. I hate peeing in a pot, and I was wearing a suit. I had just gotten my pants down when a skinny guy came out of his house. I heard him gun his motor, then he rode out of his garage on a *Harley!*

I ducked down as he roared past me, and stayed down until I heard Doyle go by. I followed them down the canyon. It was hard to brake and accelerate with my pants around my ankles. Harley turned onto Sunset and went a few miles . . . to The Velvet Swing parking lot.

I parked at the far end of the lot. A stripper walked by the car and saw me with my pants down. "I got the time if you got the money."

I pulled up my pants and lowered my voice. "No thanks." When she was gone, I grabbed my camera and pointed my telephoto lens at Harley. He approached a tattooed thug. It was a drug deal and Harley was buying. They did some blow while the bouncer stood guard. I didn't get it. What was Mike doing with a junkie?

Harley got back on his bike and took off. Doyle got out of the Lexus and staggered toward the bouncer. I was too far away to hear what he was saying. Doyle keeled over. He was on his back, unable to move. The bouncer and the thug were staring down at him. I jumped out of my car and ran over. Doyle's body was rigid and he couldn't speak. The bouncer nudged him with his foot. "Is he wasted or what?"

When Doyle didn't respond, I realized what was wrong. He was having a stroke. I called an ambulance. When they arrived, I said I was Doyle's brother so I could ride with him. We sped to the hospital, siren blaring. The paramedic took Doyle's vitals. I held Doyle's hand. He was barely conscious. One side of his mouth was paralyzed. He opened his eyes and looked at the odd little man holding his hand. "Who ah you?"

I took off my wig. My head was filled with pin curls, but I was unmistakably me. Doyle looked like he would stroke again. "Ridleh?!" His eyes rolled back in his head.

I explained to the paramedic. "He can't accept having a gay brother."

Doyle was in the ER. I was in the waiting room. I had taken out the pin curls and my hair was a frenzied bouffant. There was heavyset gay guy checking me out. He waved with his bare foot. "I sprained my ankle." He pointed with his toes. "I like your cute little suit."

I didn't want to lead him on. "My partner picked it out."

The updates on Doyle began to improve. There was some paralysis, but no cognitive impairment. The nurse told me my brother was lucky I acted so quickly, there could have been a lot more damage. That planted an idea in my head. "Please tell him what you just said."

It would be hours before they moved Doyle to his own room, so I closed my eyes to take a nap. The ace bandage squashing my breasts was starting to itch. I kept scratching my chest. The gay guy was trying to interpret the gesture. He scratched his chest suggestively. I went to the bathroom to remove the bandage. When I returned to the waiting room the gay guy was fascinated by the two large mounds bouncing under the Brooks Brother's shirt.

"Whoa, Nellie, are you male or female?"

"Both."

"A hermaphrodite?"

"Yes." Happily, that wasn't his thing.

A few hours later, the morning nurse woke me and told me they'd taken my brother to his room. I went to cardiology to grab Ronald before his first surgery. He snickered at my appearance. "A woman your age should wear a bra."

"This is a disguise."

"At least you don't stink."

"Do you recognize the suit? Stella wore it the day he became a man."

"Why did you page me?" I dragged him to Doyle's hospital room. "Who the hell is he to you?"

"Someone I want in my debt."

Ronald called in a neurological consultant, and Doyle got excellent care. He had a limp and poor balance, but they predicted he'd walk reasonably well over time. The left side of his mouth was partially paralyzed, so the insults came out garbled. "Uck you, Ridleh."

"Uck you, Oyle." He hated my sympathy, so I kept it light. I asked if there was anyone I should notify. There were no friends, no family. I was all he had. He needed me, and I needed him. But I didn't tell him why.

Doyle was going to get me my license. I needed six thousand hours working for an established investigator. Doyle would be my mentor, at least on paper. The state of California didn't need to know it was a sham. I decided not to tell Doyle my plan until I had more leverage. I went to the hospital every day. He was ornery, but relieved to see me. I persuaded him to let me be his legs, and mouth, while he was recovering.

Doyle told me what he knew about Harley. His name was Rusty Savage. He was Jessica's ex-boyfriend and "manager." Rusty discovered her working at a Dairy Queen in Fresno. They moved to LA and her career took off. She was getting hot and he was getting stoned. When Mike came along, she dumped him. Rusty lost his meal ticket.

Doyle paused and I filled in the blank—"Rusty was blackmailing Mike."

"Duuuh," Doyle said. I didn't understand him. "*Duh!*" he repeated. Even when I got something right, it was my bad. He continued uninterrupted. Rusty threatened to tell Mike's wife about the affair with Jessica. When Doyle saw me following Mike, he thought I was in on it. Then he found out I was some dumb would-be detective. Well, this would-be detective *would be* a detective, and ucking Doyle would help me get licensed.

I put Rusty's picture on the murder board. He was Viggo Mortensen sexy. Chiseled and lean, long hair, dangerous eyes. Doyle said Mike had paid Rusty over a hundred grand. Most of it was already gone. Rusty had a drug habit and he was a gambler, running big tabs at casinos. His car had been repossessed, he wasn't paying his rent. Soon he'd be evicted and harder to find, so I decided to pay Rusty a visit.

Going undercover was like playing a part. I got to act. I drove up Wonderland Avenue, rehearsing my lines. It was late morning. I wanted to catch Rusty before he got high. I rang the bell, twice. Rusty finally opened the door. He was half-asleep, no shirt, low-slung jeans he was still zipping up. He looked at me, didn't like what he saw, so I launched into my monologue.

"I'm a location scout, and I think your house might work for a movie we're shooting. It would only be one day, and we'd pay you five thousand dollars. It would be under-the-table, we don't want to deal with the city and pull the permits. It's a small crew. We'd be very careful."

Rusty bit. "I'd want to be paid in cash."

"Understood. I just need to come in and take a few pictures to show the director."

Rusty hesitated. I fed his ego. "Are you an actor?"

"No."

"You should be. You remind me of Viggo Mortensen." Rusty let me inside.

There were photographs of Jessica on every wall, including a giant blow-up that hung over the couch. "What a beautiful girl," I said.

"Yeah." He stared at her picture like a junkie in need of a fix.

"Does she live here?" I asked.

His dangerous eyes settled on me. "She doesn't come with the house."

There was lipstick on a wine glass and a platform pump under the coffee table. Maybe Jessica was here. I kept my cool and took a few pictures of the house.

"Can I see the bedroom?" I followed Rusty down the hall. The bedroom door was open. A leggy blonde was getting dressed. It wasn't Jessica.

Rusty got rid of the blonde. "She was just leaving."

That was news to her. She picked up her purse and headed out. "Call me later."

Rusty stuck out his hand. "Write down your number." She wrote her number on his hand. I took some pictures of the bedroom. One shot included the blonde and Rusty blowing her off—the poor man's version of the girl he lost. That picture was all I needed to know about Rusty Savage. He was cruel. And he was still hung up on Jessica.

I decided I should get out of there. I took a few more pictures and said I'd call when the director made a decision. Rusty got antsy, he needed that five grand. He stopped me at the door. "Don't you want my number?" I stuck out my hand, and he wrote down his number with all the eagerness of the blonde.

I drove to the hospital to update Doyle. He was dressed and ready to go home. He was leaving against doctor's orders. "I'm not going to thysical therapy with all those droolers." An orderly tried to get him in a wheelchair. Doyle limped down the corridor in a lopsided gallop. "Uck you." He still had trouble with his Fs.

Doyle's house was chaotic. Spy equipment everywhere, both cutting edge and old school. Rows of filing cabinets and ugly utilitarian furniture. The kitchen was bare, no food, just liquor. Doyle got in his bed and noticed the phone number on my hand. I tried to impress him, telling him how I got inside Rusty's house. In the middle of my brag, Doyle fell asleep. He was drooling out of the paralyzed side of his mouth. He opened one eye. "You done good."

I stocked Doyle's kitchen with healthy food, including blueberries, which are good for a brain rewiring itself after a stroke. I made him a green drink. Doyle did a spit take to rival Watson's, with only one side of his mouth. He called a pizza place and ordered everything he shouldn't eat. He knew the delivery boy and hid when he arrived. Doyle didn't want anyone to see him impaired. Except for me. "Who the uck cares what you think?" I had reverted to asshole status because of my misplaced nutritional advice.

Watson was manning the fort, and my mother, while I catered to Doyle. I had a vested interest in him staying in business until I got my license. He needed to believe I knew what I was doing. I told him about Whitey and the missing money. My stint with Amanda and hearing Kip say he was sick of lying for her. Doyle said that was worth pursuing. I was sucking him in, convincing him I could be useful. He hadn't insulted me in over an hour so I went for it—I told him I wanted him to help me get my license.

He laughed at me. "No ucking way."

"Listen, motherucker, you need me right now. And I need something from you."

"I work alone."

"Our arrangement would only be on paper. I'd be behind my stenciled door, working my own cases. The state of California needs to think I spent six thousand hours under your wing. But I won't be anywhere near your wing. After you're on your feet, I'll make myself scarce."

Doyle closed his eyes like he was thinking it over. I realized he was asleep. I sat there watching him drool. Then I got out my iPhone and made a video of Doyle drooling. When he woke up, I showed him the video. "Help me get my license or this goes viral."

Doyle gave me a lopsided smile. The student was sticking it to the master. "Okay."

"Only five thousand nine hundred and ninety-nine hours to go."

16

UNHAPPILY EVER AFTER

So many suspects, so little time. Doyle told me to focus on Amanda. I had to act fast, she was going on a press junket. I put in a few calls that went unreturned. So I devised a plan to accidentally run into Amanda at Olga's. I wanted to catch her off-guard. The Olga solution worked on many levels. I needed a nutritional kick in the ass. My detecting and my diet were overlapping, making it a legitimate expense. But I would only bill my client for half the session.

Olga greeted me in her thick Russian accent. "Your complexion tells me you have been bad." I confessed my high-glycemic sins. She cleansed me with tea and delivered me from evil. "Sugar is the devil and he takes many forms—candy, cake, and the hidden ones like white bread and pasta that turn to glucose in your blood."

I hung my head. "Mostly he appears to me as ice cream."

Olga tipped my face toward the light. "When do you succumb?"

"When I'm anxious or stressed."

The road to salvation was through my nose. Olga poured vanilla extract on a cotton ball. The scent is calming and curbs the lust for sweets. "It is not just memories of baking cookies that are evoked, even animals are soothed by the scent of vanilla." She gave me a whiff and then stuck the cotton ball under her cat's nose. I swear I saw the cat smile.

Years of sinning had depleted my neurotransmitters. I was to eat serotonin boosters to improve my mood. "Salmon and walnuts for omega-3 oils. And yogurt! Ninety percent of our serotonin is produced in the gut. Every spoonful is a tangy little tranquilizer." She grabbed my midriff. "You will get rid of this spare tire by eating yogurt. Mother Science has declared it the most slimming of all foods." I shoveled the full-fat yogurt into my mouth. Olga doesn't approve of low-fat or nonfat dairy, which has less benefit, more sugar, and no taste.

"Fend off the devil with slow carbs, which take longer to digest. Steel-cut oats, brown rice, sweet potatoes. They diminish your craving for the carbs that kill. And beans—tiny pearls of antioxidants, protein and fiber. Eat one-half cup every day."

Olga surprised me by dangling a cookie in my direction. "If you must eat the rapidly digested suicide carbs, have protein first to retard their absorption and fight inflammation. Perhaps a glass of organic milk from a grass-fed cow."

I waved the cookie away. On my one hundred and twentieth birthday I can have a cookie to celebrate. Good for me! I don't hear that very often inside my head. Maybe it was the vanilla talking— talking to myself—usually I was more judgmental. Facing down a cookie is not curing cancer or solving a case, but I was proud of myself.

I got out my wallet and wrote Olga a check. When she wasn't looking, I wedged the wallet between the cushions of her velvet sofa. A kiss on both cheeks and she sent me on my way. "Sweet potatoes taste better than Prozac and the carotenoids are good for your skin."

That was on a Wednesday. I knew Amanda had a standing appointment with Olga every Thursday, so I went back the next day. I waited until Amanda's session was almost over and rang the doorbell. I apologized to Olga, "I think I left my wallet here."

Amanda's serotonin levels plunged when she saw me. "What are you doing here?"

"I'm an Olga devotee. I couldn't survive without my green drinks." I went to the sofa to search for my wallet and pretended relief when I found it. "Here it is. I didn't realize it was gone until I went to Whole Foods to buy Pavel's Russian yogurt." Olga smiled beatifically, I could be saved. I think Amanda frowned, her Botoxed brow had no mobility.

Olga's next client arrived. She fluttered like a mother swan as she walked me and Amanda to the door. Olga stood beneath the Romanov crest, waving us off. "Studies show that friendship extends longevity as much as fish oil."

Amanda didn't know how to deal with me. She opted for chummy. "I'm glad I ran into you. I'm doing a movie, playing an undercover cop. You go undercover. You could help me understand the character. If you have time, why don't you come over?"

I accepted the invitation and tried to make nice as she walked away. "You still look great from behind."

I was impressed with the job George did on the house. Amanda gave me a tour, taking some shots at George's bogus assistant. "Ecru or eggshell?" she said mockingly. She'd be bitchy, then treat me like her new best friend. You never knew what was coming. Maybe that's how she kept Mike's interest. She certainly kept mine.

We talked about Olga. I admitted my nutritional lapses. Amanda had none. We went to the kitchen and had an early dinner. Amanda explained, "If you have dinner by six and don't eat another bite, you are guaranteed to lose weight. Then take a walk and it gets burned for energy instead of turning to fat."

We went to her home gym and got on parallel treadmills. Amanda increased her speed. I couldn't keep up. "You're so disciplined."

"I have to be." She huffed and puffed as she complained about the burdens of celebrity. "Losing your looks is harder if you're famous. Tabloids love to run an ugly shot. The red-carpet reviews that pick you apart."

"Thank God I get to age anonymously." The truth was, I wanted her problems. The loss of fame was better than never achieving it.

Amanda increased her speed. "When you trade on your looks,

every year you're worth a little less. A beautiful woman is like a flower that blooms briefly. You have to cash in while you're in bloom."

"In some cultures they revere the elderly," I said lamely.

"They may revere them but they don't want to fuck them."

We returned to the kitchen, and Amanda made us some tea. Her violet eyes narrowed as she studied me. "I'm not sure I can play an undercover cop. What is it like to deceive the people you befriend? You'd have to be a really good liar."

"Kind of like being an actress."

"Are you a good liar, Billie?" A cold smile. "*Billy Liar*. Did you ever see that?"

"Great movie," I mumbled into my tea. I hadn't seen it.

Her eyes narrowed again. "All that flattering of my ass. Did you go home and laugh at my insecurity? What are the private moments of someone undercover?"

"Mostly I went home and ate ice cream."

Kip did a demonic Desi Arnaz impression as he entered the kitchen. "Honey, I'm home." He was shooting a sci-fi flick and was still wearing his makeup. His face was a black and white grid. And he was drunk. "I have an early call, and this crap is too hard to take off and put on again. I'm not spending three hours in the makeup chair. I'll sleep sitting up." His bloodshot eyes landed on me. "Why is this person in my kitchen?"

"Billie is helping me research a role," Amanda told him.

"You're playing a lying little bitch?"

"An undercover cop," said the lying little bitch.

Kip smiled so wide he cracked his grid. "Amanda is not playing an undercover cop."

I looked at Amanda. She held my gaze unapologetically. "I want to know why you were spying on me. What was it you wanted to know?"

"Who killed Mike."

The mere mention of Mike's name shook them both. Amanda came undone. "And what did you find out?"

"Not enough."

Kip seethed. "Dead or alive I can't get that prick out of my life!"

126

Amanda welled up. "No, no, I can't cry. I don't want bags under my eyes."

Her tears enraged Kip. He went to the fridge and opened the door. "Let the hunger games begin." He grabbed all the fattening food he could carry and stuck it in the microwave. I could smell the fried chicken, mac and cheese, biscuits, brownies, cookies. Amanda looked longingly at the forbidden foods as they went around and around on the carousel. Ding!

Kip sat at the island, taking big sloppy bites. Gravy dripped down his chin creating little rivulets in his grid. "These are Amanda's favorite foods." He got up and chewed in her face. "Best biscuit I ever ate."

Amanda grabbed her purse and took out a bottle of pills. She poured a glass of wine and took two pills. "Colonel Sanders be damned."

Kip slurped more gravy. "Amanda dines on diet pills." She took out another bottle of pills. "And tranqs to deal with her checkered mate."

Amanda took a tranq. "You will not make me fat and you will not drive me crazy."

Kip took the chicken leg out of his mouth and waved it at his hungry wife. "Bad guys don't have to be pretty. But forty-something leading ladies are stuck in a leafy green hell."

He kept eating and she kept taking pills. It degenerated into a food fight. Amanda threw a brownie at Kip that I caught and ate. I had no diet pills, so I had no restraint. High-calorie missiles were lobbed over the island. I would duck and nibble, eating all the goodies I could catch. I was stuffed and wanted to go home. So I steered the battle back to Mike.

Amanda took another tranq. "Who do you think killed him?"

You, I was thinking. But I gave her my standard, "I suspect everyone."

She was swinging between her uppers and downers. Her moods changing in mid-sentence. She smiled at me, "Billie," then she lashed out, "you think I did it. Which proves what a rotten detective you are." More tears. "Mike was the love of my life. I'd sooner kill myself."

Kip lost it. "I am your husband!"

Amanda was affectionate, "I'm so sorry, Kippy." Then she turned on him, "I can't stand to look at you anymore."

"You made me ugly!" Kip clawed the paint off his face, he was half-checked and half-flesh. "*Amanda was driving the night of the accident!*"

Amanda tried to shut him up, but Kip was out of control. "She was upset because she wanted to be with Mike. She ran into a pole and I paid the price! Everyone thought she was heroic for pulling me from the car. She was trying to hide the fact that she was driving! And she was drunk! What would that do to her career? What about *my* fucking career?!"

Amanda wailed. "He threatened to tell the world what I did if I ever left him."

"I've lied for you long enough!"

Bells went off inside my head—this was the lie Kip was sick of telling.

Amanda shook me like a rag doll. "You can't tell anyone, you can't tell!"

I had to get out of there. I waited until they were attacking each other and I ran. I escaped unharmed and three pounds heavier.

Just because the lie wasn't about the murder didn't mean Amanda, or her very angry husband, did not kill Mike. They both remained suspects.

I didn't tell Felicia about my deal with Doyle. It made me look like an amateur. But I told her about Kip and Amanda. The affair with Mike went back at least ten years. Amanda couldn't leave Kip, he would have exposed her. But that didn't mean Mike wanted to marry her. Felicia told me to keep digging.

The truth about the car accident got out. Kip did the talk-show circuit, busting his wife and promoting his movies. It doubled his asking price, and Amanda's. The worst they could get her on was a ten-year-old DUI. Her lawyers kept her out of court, and her agents made more deals. They each did endless interviews talking about the atrocities of their marriage. They were addicted to fame and only relevant in relation to each other. So they stayed together.

17
LACTIC ACID

Doyle gave me his take on Kip and Amanda. "Mike was always giving them money when times were tough. He probably knew Amanda was driving and felt some responsibility. He cleared his conscience by writing a check. That's how rich men sleep at night. You do enough damage, the money won't cover it and you get killed." Doyle closed his eyes and soon he was drooling. I was his Ambien. Most healing happens while you sleep, I was doing him a favor.

Doyle's brain had become a personal quest. It wasn't just the license. It was daddy stuff—I needed to save him. I had physical therapists come to the house. He'd limp around and curse me out. I hid healthy ingredients in all the crap he ate. I popped fish oil capsules and drizzled them on his pizza, omega-3s are crucial for the brain.

"Why does this pepperoni smell like *fish*?" It was his first F since the stroke. Doyle was delighting in his Fs. "What the *fuck* are you smiling about?"

Doyle said we needed to *focus* on Rusty. I put in a call, posing as the location scout. I told Rusty the director didn't want to use the house. Then I asked about Jessica. I said the director wanted to audition the beautiful girl I had seen in the pictures. Rusty's response was a coked-up rant about all the men who wanted her. If Rusty was that revealing with a stranger, what was he saying to people he knew?

I wanted to tap Rusty's cell phone. Doyle said it couldn't be done. I said I'd find a way. He gave me his usual eye roll. I slipped vitamin D into his enchilada and took off, determined to prove the eye roll wrong.

To tap a cell phone you need to have the actual phone. You get on the Internet, go to a website that sells a monitoring program and download it onto the phone. The person can't tell his phone is tapped. You can monitor his calls and messages on your computer. Most people spy on a spouse or their kid, someone they live with. I didn't have access to Rusty's phone. But I had Hacker.

I made him a meatloaf with grass-fed beef, which has as much omega-3 as salmon. What was good for Doyle's brain was good for Hacker's and for mine. I decided to go All-Olga. My memory improved and so did my mood. Watson was so impressed she had a green drink. It still tasted like the bitter elixir she once spit out. But you don't take supplements and complain about the taste— "My vitamin B tastes like shit." Olga says getting nutrients from food is more beneficial than the synthesized version in pills. Drinking this cocktail of health is a badge of courage.

Hacker was able to tap Rusty's phone. I went back to Doyle's place with my laptop, and we listened to a few minutes of Rusty calling his dealer. Doyle's partially paralyzed jaw dropped. "The dingbat detective may be an asset."

We listened to hours of Rusty's phone calls. Scoring drugs, fending off bill collectors, placing bets. He left rambling messages for Jessica. The last message was an angry diatribe about her and Mike. "How could you fuck that guy? For a car and a house! Now that he's dead, why don't I move in? You too good for me now? Call me back, or I'm coming over."

Jessica finally called him back. She was pleading with him to let her go. "It's over, Rusty. It was over a long time ago. And not because of Mike. You need help."

"What I need is some Fresno pussy."

Jessica started to cry. "If you don't leave me alone, I'll call the police."

Rusty hung up. He was afraid of the police. And I was afraid for Jessica. I was surprised that I felt protective of the beautiful blonde who got all the men. I understood Amanda's jealousy. She wilted, so Mike got himself a long-stemmed replacement in full bloom. I felt like compost. I sprinkled turmeric on Doyle's Big Mac and went home.

I got a disturbing call of my own. Gary said our lawyer, Mickey, had some papers for me to sign. We were selling some property to pay our legal fees. We still had property? That was news to me. I didn't trust him, so I had Hacker tap Gary's phone.

My blood boiled as I monitored his calls. Mickey and Gary were deciding how to tell me that I was selling a boat I never knew I had. Our creditors' lawyers insisted the spouse at the time of purchase sign the bill of sale. The rest of the calls were equally maddening. Lilah had a great time last night and would love to play doctor again. Naomi could play doctor on Saturday night. But there was something even more disturbing.

Vera, the cosmetic chemist and discarded mistress, called Gary three times. "Didn't you get my messages? Why didn't you call me back? Are you too busy seducing other women on *Doctor Feel Good*?!" Apparently, that was the name of my boat.

Gary was downright rude to her. "Stop calling me, Vera. Move on with your life." She would cry, then another chorus of accusation and vitriol. There is no woman more scorned than the other woman when she is dumped.

All the problems with the anti-aging cream began after Gary ended the affair. I carved out a section of the murder board and started writing down batch numbers and dates. No one ever thought of tampering. The independent lab said no suspicious ingredients had been introduced. But Vera was a chemist. She would know how to tamper and not be detected. All she had to do was change the concentrations. More lactic acid with less squalene and shea to oppose it. No one's face would fall off and prompt a criminal investigation. Just enough swelling and irritation to derail a product line that was about to launch.

I knew in my gut that I was right. But I had to prove it without alerting Vera. And without Gary knowing I tapped his phone. When Gary gave me the bill of sale to sign, I yelled like the boat was new news. I brought up his crimes against our marriage—the affairs with other women, including Vera. "Do you still see her?" I asked plaintively.

"Not if I can help it. She calls me all the time . . . " His voice trailed off. He gave me the most sincere apology of our divorce. "I'm sorry, Billie. I get a little sorrier every day."

I savored the moment and then hit him with my theory about Vera the Tamptress. He reminded me there was no evidence of tampering. I reminded him I was a dick and knew what I was talking about. She had motive up the ying yang, a rejected ying yang, and she had opportunity.

I told Gary I would sign the bill of sale if he got me the jars of anti-aging cream that his over-exfoliated patients had returned. He could only find six jars, but that was enough. He demanded to know why I wanted the jars. I took a long stage wait. I knew he would ridicule me, and I wanted him to remember that when I turned out to be right.

"I'm dusting for prints."

He ridiculed right on cue. "*Dusting for prints*. Do you hear yourself?"

I got out the fifty-dollar fingerprint kit I bought at Under Cover. Watson assisted me. I took the tiny brush and dusted black powder on the prints that were on the jars. I stuck transparent tape on the powder and lifted each print. I stuck the tape on the white ID cards that came with the kit. As I lifted the prints, I explained my thinking.

"Vera wasn't on the production line. She was the chemist. There is no reason her prints should be on these jars. Unless she went to the lab in the dark of night and did some tampering."

Watson asked the obvious question. "How you gonna know which prints are hers?"

"Gary is going to take her to dinner, ply her with wine and bring me the glass."

Gary refused. But I had not signed the bill of sale on the boat. I promised to sign as soon as he got me that wine glass. Gary called

Vera and made a date. He practically had to sleep with her to get it, but he got me the glass.

The prints on the wine glass matched the prints on the jars! Nothing feels better than one-upping your ex with the other woman's fingerprints.

Now we had to confront Vera. There was no financial gain in going to the cops. My goal was to squeeze the lab. But we only had leverage if their chemist's malicious tampering was kept secret. They would not want to risk losing customers if it got out.

I had Gary call Vera and make another date. She didn't know it, but I would be with him. And I'd be wearing a wire. "Be seductive, don't tip her off," I told him. Gary didn't need any coaching. Vera told him to be at her place at eight.

The wire was part of my spy shit arsenal. It was a digital voice recorder attached to a tiny microphone. I taped the recorder to my waist and ran the wire through my bra so that the mic was lodged between my breasts. I put on a V-neck sweater and did a sound check. "Testing, testing—"

"Make sure them big-ass tatas don't muffle the sound," Watson warned.

I reached inside my sweater and hit the playback button on the recorder. "Testing, testing . . . Make sure them big-ass tatas don't muffle the sound." It was clear as a bell. I was wired.

We arrived at Vera's apartment an hour late. I wanted her angry and vulnerable, afraid he wasn't coming. If she was emotional, she'd be less censored. Gary rang the bell. I stood behind him, hidden from view.

Vera opened the door. "I want you," she said as she pulled him close. While they were kissing, I ducked inside. Vera was wearing a sexy negligee. Candles were glowing all over the room. Down and dirty R & B with a raunchy male vocal was on the stereo. There was an open bottle of wine, Vera was tipsy with anticipation. A trail of rose petals led to the bedroom. It was reminiscent of my pitiful fishnet seduction. I almost felt guilty for setting her up.

Gary pulled out of the kiss and Vera saw me. "Hello, Vera," I said after she stopped screaming.

Vera turned to Gary. "Did she follow you?"

"We came here together," Gary said.

"I don't understand. I thought you split up."

"We did," I assured her. "Then the idiot wife became a private detective. I know what you did."

Vera raised her hands in mock surrender. "Okay, you got me, we had an affair."

"I'm not here because you screwed my husband. I'm here because you screwed my company."

Vera looked at Gary. "I don't know what she's talking about."

Gary shot back— "You tampered with the anti-aging cream and buried my brand!"

"*Our* brand," I reminded him.

Vera tried to deny it, but Gary cut her off. "We found your fingerprints on the jars." I love how the ridiculer said *we*. But I wanted to provoke her, so I let him take the lead.

A saxophone wailed on the stereo as Vera attacked Gary. "It's all your fault—you drove me to it! I was a *chemist*, not some disposable piece of ass! Throwing me over for some infomercial model!"

The throbbing music was building to a climax. I was afraid Vera's confession would be obscured. I moved toward her, sticking out my chest so she'd be closer to the microphone. "You tampered with the product."

"He tampered with my heart so I struck back!"

"By destroying Sontag Skincare."

Vera pushed me away. "Yes, you stupid cow!" Her hand hit the playback button on the recorder . . .

"I want you," Vera heard herself say. She heard herself scream. Then she heard me say, "Hello, Vera." I desperately tried to turn off the recorder. "Did she follow you?"

What followed was a stream of expletives at Gary and me when she realized I was wired. A wine glass flew at his head as we ran for the door. I grabbed the glass in case we needed more prints.

Vera disappeared after that night. No forwarding address, nada. But why go after her? There was no money in it. I felt sorry for her. And grateful in a weird way. I was happier in my new life. I might not be the private eye I am today if it hadn't been for Vera the idiot chemist.

We went to the lab and presented our evidence to the owner and his lawyer. I played Vera's confession with its suggestive R & B soundtrack. A deep male voice sang dirty Do Me lyrics as Vera unloaded. I pulsed to the beat as we made our case.

The lab's chemist deliberately destroyed our company, something they would not want their customers to know. They threatened to ruin Gary's reputation if he tried to ruin theirs. He used Vera to create his product, and then he dumped her and his wife of thirty years for the infomercial model. Women don't like their derms to be dirtbags. Gary would lose his patients and what credibility he had left. Neither side wanted the fight to go public, so we hammered out a deal. They agreed to pay all the legal bills and settle the lawsuits in exchange for our silence.

We walked out of that office with no more debt. Every now and then, I dance to Vera's confession to celebrate the win.

Gary was impressed I had figured it out. We go back a long way and that includes a lot of shorthand. "Come on, Gary, give it to me."

He knew exactly what that meant. "You were right."

I have "rightitis." That's what Margo calls it, she has it too. Most people do, but mine is acute. It probably comes from having a mother who had to be right. She was bigger than me, which rendered me wrong. Now I need to be right with everyone—my kid, my ex, my BFF, suspects, strangers, Doyle. That's what I want on my tombstone: "I Was Right." Maybe it should be: "She Was Right." But someone might think "she" was my mother. By the time I'm a hundred and twenty who's going to remember my mother?

18
SAY IT AIN'T SO

Sometimes I get it so wrong. Doyle got a call from an informant at the LAPD. Sarah had been arrested for killing Mike. I was stunned. This woman was my friend, a kindred first wife. There but for the grace of cowardice go I. When Gary cheated on me, I wanted to kill him. But I shot him with a camera instead of a gun.

I went to the police station to confirm it with Logan. "Are you okay?" he asked. What a loaded question, I hadn't seen him since the morning-after fiasco with Franky.

I realized his question pertained to Sarah. "She was a suspect, but I didn't see this coming. You're sure she did it?"

"She confessed." Logan didn't treat me like the disillusioned amateur I was, he treated me with respect. "No one knew this case better than you. It might be helpful for you to hear her story."

The Bad Cop was in the interrogation room with Sarah. Logan and I were observing them through the two-way mirror. She cried when she said why she did it. "I still loved him. That didn't stop just because he left me. But it turned into something else. Shame, I guess. Everywhere I went, even when I was alone, I was ashamed. Then he told me Felicia was pregnant. He was going have a child with someone else. A child that wasn't broken like mine. Mike asked me to marry him three times before I said yes. How do you humiliate someone you used to love? I couldn't take it anymore. I didn't mean to hurt him. I loved him."

When her confession was on the record, a female cop escorted Sarah out of the room. I saw her briefly before they took her away. I said what I felt. "I'm so sorry it was you."

She couldn't look at me. "Me too." Sarah walked off in handcuffs. *Handcuffs*. I liked her so much. How could this be?

The thing that did me in was the Bad Cop's regret. "Sometimes I hate my job."

Logan walked me to my car. A cop came running up to report on another case. "The victim took two in the chest, the perp was a banger." Logan took it in stride and we continued on.

I didn't get it. "How do you do this every day?"

"Some days are harder than others." I saw decades of hard days on his face. The broad shoulders were for show. I didn't want to part. But I had to update my client.

Felicia was very shaken when I told her about Sarah. She put her hand over her mouth, as if to silence her thoughts, then they tumbled out. "I broke up their marriage."

I tried to console her. "Mike had never been faithful. This wasn't your fault."

"You don't have to remind me that he was unfaithful." She wasn't angry at me, she was angry at him. And guilty. The widow was the other woman. She gets the guy, she gets pregnant, and he gets killed by the wife he left behind.

I promised myself I'd never look at a married man again. Logan and I would have no more pie. No more walking me to my car. Mrs. Logan didn't deserve that. I wondered what she was like. She had to be younger than me. And certainly a better person, I said to myself.

Felicia didn't hire me to find out who murdered Mike. I was supposed to find out who he loved. It didn't even make sense anymore. But I needed the job and Felicia seemed to need me, so my investigation continued. It was her way of coping with the loss. Her perfectly manicured hand with the big diamond ring came to rest on her belly. "This baby is all I have left of him." What a weight that kid would carry.

Watson was still there when I got home. She sympathized with Sarah. "A man can drive you batshit. I put Nair on my boyfriend's johnson while he was sleeping. He thought twice about getting a friendly BJ from the neighbor lady after that." If only I'd been that inventive with Gary.

I went to the murder board and drew a circle around Sarah's picture—a picture I had taken when I was following Mike. I looked at her sad eyes as she looked at him. How could I not see the degree of her pain?

Watson went home, and I went to bed depressed. I hated that my instincts were so wrong. All the confidence I felt after busting Vera had been eroded. I started to question my new career. I was a mediocre actress, and now I was a mediocre detective. I was outstandingly mediocre. Never a beauty, a discarded wife, a deficient mother.

I was trapped inside my wrinkled skin with my chief detractor. You are a failure! It's so strange, the way we talk to ourselves. *You* is second person, grammatically speaking. I responded to myself— Who are you to talk, you're as big a failure as *me*. That is the first person—me, myself, the idiot I. We'd been having this dialogue ever since I could talk. We finally fell asleep and had a dream. In my dreams I am united, there is only one of me contending with all of *them*—the third persons.

Sarah and I were sitting in her kitchen. "I fooled you," she said. I didn't get mad, I got hungry. We were eating kale ice cream. It was bittersweet and I couldn't get enough. Danny sat down and started banging on the table, trying to get my attention.

I woke up abruptly. Danny was banging on my door. "Billie, let me in!" When I let him in, he was as agitated as I'd ever seen him. "My mother's in jail!" I tried to calm him down, but he was out of control. "They think she killed my father!" In the midst of all the yelling, he looked at me accusingly. "Why do you have tape on your forehead?"

I peeled off the tape and explained my eleven lines. Danny went off again about his mother. "Why is this happening? She didn't do it."

"She confessed," I told him as gently as I could.

Danny grabbed me. "She didn't do it!"

He was so intense it begged a question. "How do you know that, Danny?"

"I just do," he said angrily. I looked at his wrist and my heart stopped. Danny was wearing Mike's missing watch. If this kid killed his father, killing me wouldn't even count. But he seemed to regard me as an ally in proving Sarah's innocence.

I placated and probed very cautiously. "We should go to the police and you can tell them what you think." I looked out the window. "It's still dark outside. What time is it?"

Danny looked at the watch. "Three–thirty."

He didn't try to hide it, so I casually asked, "Isn't that Mike's watch?"

"Is that why you're so nervous?" Danny couldn't read people's emotions but my shaking was a dead giveaway.

I faked a smile. "I remember how much he liked it."

"I'm smarter than you, don't treat me like a fool."

"Okay. How did you get the watch?"

"I stole it." He avoided eye contact, talking to my eleven lines. "The night before my dad died, I slept over at his house. He told me Felicia was going to have a baby." Danny started to rock forward and back. "I was angry and that made him angry. He didn't want to upset Felicia. He was always so worried about Felicia, what about me? In the morning, when he was in the shower, I took the watch. Then I walked home. I was going to make him get me a car in exchange for the watch." He stopped rocking and looked me in the eye. "At first I was afraid to wear it. But even if I stole it, his watch belongs to me now. My father is dead."

I was calm and deliberate. "Did your mother see you wearing that watch?"

"What does the watch have to do with my mother?! She didn't steal it. She didn't do anything wrong." He was rocking again. "Why is she in jail? She didn't kill him!"

"Maybe she thinks you did."

I took Danny to see Logan. Danny was frantic. "Tell my mother I stole the watch. Tell her I didn't hurt my dad, I just took the watch." When they brought Sarah to see him, Danny kept yelling, "Tell them you didn't do it, you were protecting me, tell them the truth!" As her anguished son screamed of her innocence, Sarah covered her face with her manacled hands. Logan removed her handcuffs. Danny's frantic pleas continued until Sarah retracted her confession. The DA wanted to press charges against her for lying, but Logan got him to back off.

Sarah never thanked me. She was still afraid that Danny killed his father. I thought about her moving confession in the interrogation room. But loving Mike was very real and so was the hurt about losing him. The tears she shed were for her son.

Felicia confirmed that Danny slept over that night. But Mike didn't tell her his watch was missing. Maybe he thought he left it on some woman's bedside. Felicia was relieved that Sarah didn't kill Mike. Breaking up the marriage did not cause his death. His murder was still unsolved. My investigation made sense again, at least to me.

Danny's volatile behavior kept him a suspect. The police knew Mike was amending his will to include the baby. Danny got so little of his father. Stuff—the car, the printer, the watch—became the all-consuming substitute. Another child meant that Danny would only get half. And the unbroken baby would get all the love.

Danny's anger at his father was stirring my own. Husbands cheat on their wives, and the kids pay the price. I felt sorry for Danny. And Emma. It was sixty years later, and I chose this moment to admit that Murray was cheating on my mother.

I arrived at Krasny's office late and contentious. "It costs too much to park around here." I blew the first ten minutes talking about work. "One of my suspects is so angry at his father that his mother thought he murdered him. Mike's kid, Danny. You take some kind of oath, right? Nothing goes out of this room. I can talk about people and who they might have killed. Some of my suspects are celebrities."

"Let's not talk about your suspects, let's talk about you."

I threw him a dream to interpret, then got mad that he didn't bust me for stalling. I circled back to Danny. "He was so angry, it got me angry at Murray, and I didn't know why. Then I realized, after all this time . . . my father was having an affair. He wasn't just cheating on my mother. If he loved me, he wouldn't risk losing his family."

"You were angry at him and then he died—"

"I am not crying, so keep that insightful crap to yourself."

"But you already paid for parking."

"They were fighting all night. June threw his suitcase out the door. It opened up and his clothes fell out. She cried for days. He came back. But things were never the same. My mother's despair put a damper on playing horsey with daddy."

"Tell me about that."

"Murray would get down on all fours, and I'd ride around on his back, laughing my head off. 'Goody up, daddy!' No one corrected me, they thought it was cute. When I got tired, Murray would pick me up in my Dr. Denton's and carry me to bed. That was as good as childhood gets."

"How old were you when he had the affair?"

"Five. He sold insurance, so he was traveling all the time. He began to stay away longer. He hurt his back so we didn't play horsey anymore. I was too heavy. That woman he was screwing, I wonder if she had any kids."

"The anger you feel is born of something deeper. The hurt, the longing. The love."

"I'm sick of talking about him. That's all we ever do. Fuck my father."

"You wanted him all to yourself. He and your mother would go off to their room, you'd get angry and wish for them to part. It's normal to have those wishes. When they had problems, you felt like it was your fault." I looked at my watch. "Maybe that's why you're angry at me."

"Because you go home to your wife? I should move in with you. She can sleep in the guest room. We won't have sex, that would be unethical. But we can play horsey. Goody-up, Krasny." His smile was as rewarding as a ride on his back. That was the day I decided he liked me. I had found myself a very able, very expensive father.

I went to see June, to check the facts against my memory. Her gout was acting up, so she was wearing the fuzzy pink slippers I gave her for Mother's Day. She asked about my case. I told her I'd been in a food fight with Kip and Amanda. And I told her how a mother had confessed to a murder to protect her kid. June said she would have done that for me. I thanked her for the voucher and thought about who I might kill.

When I brought up my father's infidelity, June had a bout of dementia. She kept talking about her father. Grandpa had a zipper problem too. When the dementia wasn't playing, she let it taper off and gave me an answer.

"Murray was on the road a lot, and I was home with you. There was another woman. She called him one time. I believe her name was Gladys. Whenever he went away I imagined he was with her." She looked at me through her ancient, overly made-up eyes. "I will love that man till the day I die." I thought his death was my tragedy, but she missed him as much as I did.

June shuffled to the bedroom. "Come with me, Billie." She opened her closet door and had me stand on a chair. "Get me that box, way up in the corner." I handed her the cardboard box, which she treated with exquisite care. She opened the lid. Tears filled her eyes, and then they filled mine. Inside the box was a pair of Murray's brown leather shoes. They were scuffed, lived in, like the man who wore them. She gave me the shoes. "These belong to you. You didn't get enough of your daddy."

June shuffled back to the living room. Her program was about to begin. Poignant memories, lost love, nothing would come between her and the TV.

I took Murray's shoes out of the box and walked around in them, like I did when I was a kid. They were still much too big. He wasn't tall, but he had feet as big as his heart. His cheating heart, I reminded myself. No man will ever love me as much as my father. No one will light up just because I walk in the room wearing his shoes. Oh, for one more of those glorious smiles.

June fell asleep in front of the TV. As I sorted her meds, I thought about what is was like to walk in her shoes, or her slippers, with her gout and bunions. She loved Murray, more than I knew. He died and she had to raise me alone. She went from the chorus line to a desk job so I wouldn't be without my mother at night. Now I was the caretaker, the one on duty while she slept. I owed her that much.

June woke up and said she was hungry. She requested a fried peanut butter and banana sandwich like Elvis Presley used to eat. June was a Broadway baby, but she was also a big Elvis fan. "He was devoted to his mother. When she went on tour, Elvis fell on her coffin and cried, 'I lived my whole life for you.'" June sang "Love Me Tender" and sent me to the kitchen.

All she had was white bread, which I recognized as a manifestation of the devil. So I made it breadlessly. I put some organic coconut oil in a pan and let it melt. I sliced a ripe banana into long pieces and put it in the pan. I got out the Laura Scudder's peanut butter. If you store it upside down, the oil spreads through the jar, and you don't have to stir as much. I put a teaspoon of peanut butter on each slice of banana and let it simmer. A dash of salt to contrast the sweetness and five minutes later it was done. I served it to my mother hot and bubbly. She damn near came.

And it was actually good for her. Coconut oil is great for the heart, the banana has potassium, peanut butter has protein. We decided to give the desert a name. June dubbed it "Elvis" in his honor. Then she informed me, "His mother's name was Gladys. That's what made me think of the sandwich." The same name as my father's girlfriend. Maybe Murray was sleeping with Elvis Presley's mother.

When I got home, Harpo was waiting for me. That song we recorded had legs. Ten thousand downloads got him on the bill at the Downtown Lounge. And little old me, incredibly old me, would be singing backup. Harpo told me to invite all my friends so we'd have a full house. Margo did her thing, and the tiny venue was booked to capacity. Emma was torn between embarrassment and pride. She told Gary, who asked if he could come. I had Watson bring June—how many more times in her life or mine would I be onstage?

What to wear, who to be? I stood in Stella's closet trying on everyone from Britney to Cher. No one who paid a ten-dollar cover should be forced to look at my midriff. All that glittered was so un-Harpo. He wanted me. So I wore jeans and a T-shirt that said "I'm

With The Band."

There were other bands hanging around, waiting to go on. Harpo, Dog, and the two Jerrys were used to the elderly backup singer, but to all the other rockers, I was an anomaly. No weed, no Red Bull, not for me. I was high on green drinks, three in one day. Harpo had to scrape me off the ceiling, I was that nervous, inadequate, wired! Harpo was unflappable. He was high on music. "Don't hold back," he told us. "Have fun out there." Dog threw up and we went on.

I saw my mother in the audience. She yelled it out before a note was heard—"Sing out, Billie." She always said that before an audition or one of my living room performances as a child. It was my big night, and Momma June gets the laugh.

Well, sing out I did. Loud and unruly, sweating up a storm, I was transported. Harpo's rebellious gotta-dance anthem brought down the house. We got a standing O. My first one. I basked in Gary's wide-eyed *wow*. And Emma's earnest rocking out. But the best part, the one that beat the O, was Momma June's, "That's my little girl."

It's always darkest before the dawn. And brightest before the shit hits the fan. That's why I'm wary of a good time. I always think the bad times will last forever and the good is only a prelude to disaster. I went home perilously euphoric. The shit exceeded my worst expectations. My loft, my home, my new life, had been ransacked.

19
A TURKEY TO REMEMBER

I stood in the doorway, paralyzed with disbelief. My possessions were scattered across the floor. What wasn't trashed was missing— laptop, cameras, anything of any value. Stella's closet had been torn apart. Watson's desk drawers were emptied out. *Fuck You* was scribbled on the murder board. This wasn't just theft, it was malice. I ran down the hall to get Hacker. He called 911 and I called Logan. I assumed the ransacking was related to my case.

The perp climbed up the fire escape and came in through the window. The police dusted for prints. There was yellow crime-scene tape outside my door. Logan was mindful of the other cops. He was caring but professional as he took my statement. I guess Hacker called Watson. I looked up and there she was. She gave me the hug I'd hoped to get from Logan.

We talked about motive. Most of the suspects on the murder board were at Ivan's gallery for Danny's show, they knew where I lived. The intruder seemed to have a personal grudge. Vera came to mind, but I couldn't imagine her climbing the fire escape. "Maybe it was someone who hated my singing."

Logan was not amused. "Maybe you're getting too close to solving the case." I smiled, he frowned. "This isn't a game, it's dangerous. You don't have the training." He lowered his voice so the other cops wouldn't hear him. "You don't even have a license."

"I'm working for Johnny Doyle, accumulating my six thousand hours." Logan stared at me. "Doyle had a stroke. I needed a license and he needed the help."

Logan lowered his voice again. "You're good at this, you have good instincts, you get people to open up. But, Billie . . . " I love how he said my name, like we were close. Friends. I wasn't aiming for more than that. "This is way over your head. I don't want you to get hurt."

"Over my head" was like waving a red flag at a bull. The ransacking scared me, but this bull was not backing off. I let him see my fear and hid my resolve. "Okay," I said timidly.

"Don't be pissed off."

I loved that he could read me. "Okay." I walked him to the door. They were taking down the yellow tape. I asked if I could keep it. Logan nodded and the cop gave me the whole roll.

When Logan was gone, Watson said, "The Po-Po's kinda cute."

"The Po-Po's kinda married."

Watson and Hacker helped me clean up. When I moved out of Beverly Hills, I only kept what mattered. Now someone had messed with my crucial stuff. I picked up a cracked porcelain turkey and was reminded it was almost Emma's thirtieth birthday, which would fall on Thanksgiving Day. I had a menagerie of little porcelain turkeys. I counted, they were all there, all twenty-nine of them. Every year Gary gave me a turkey on Emma's birthday. I stood there holding that damaged bird. I missed being a family.

Dawn was breaking and I made Watson go home. Hacker offered me lodging, but I wanted to sleep in my familiar Beverly Hills bed. I doused it with vanilla and got under the covers. I was almost asleep, then my eyes popped open. *The sex tape!*

I had removed the video of Mike and Jessica having sex from my camera and copied it onto a DVD. I went to the credenza where I had hidden it. The DVD was gone. I was afraid to tell the cops, shooting it was illegal. No one but me and Watson knew it existed. Then I remembered hearing footsteps in the backyard the night I shot it.

I didn't know what to do, so I went to Doyle. He said not to tell anyone about the sex tape. I couldn't even be sure when it went missing. He was more upset about the break-in. "It's time you got yourself a piece." Doyle sent me to his friend at Gun City.

Gus pressed a buzzer and let me in the store. He weighed three hundred pounds and had the fattest neck I'd ever seen. "You looking for a pistol or a revolver?"

"What's the difference?" I asked.

Gus wheezed as he looked at me, why would Doyle send him this ignorant skirt? He opened the case and took out a gun. "This is a revolver. The round cylinder holds five bullets." He spun the cylinder. "See, it revolves every time you shoot it."

I had never held a gun before. I'm morally opposed to them.

"You got tiny hands," Gus observed. "A revolver is smaller, but the trigger is harder to pull." He took a larger gun out of the case. "This is a semiautomatic *pistol.*" He let me hold it. "Easier trigger action, less kick—a gun tips up when you shoot it. The magazine holds ten bullets." He took it out of the handle and shoved it back in.

"Why do they call it a magazine?"

"They just do."

"I don't like the look of a pistol. A revolver is more feminine. Maybe it's generational. I want something Barbara Stanwyck might have carried."

"How do you know Doyle again?"

"I'm his associate." He looked at me blankly. "I'm a dick," I clarified.

"Seriously, is this some kind of joke?" He chuckled hopefully, then it petered out.

I pointed to a pearl-handled revolver inside the case. "That one looks nice."

Gus took out the revolver. I knew it the minute I held it. This was my gun. It was a snubnose .38. "What does the .38 mean?"

"The ammo—the size of the bullets. You want hollow-point, they expand inside the body."

"That seems so mean."

"You're shooting somebody and you're worried about mean?"

"Regular bullets will be fine."

It came to five hundred dollars with Doyle's discount. But I couldn't have my gun, not yet. In California there's a mandatory ten-day wait. A cooling off period. I filled out all the paperwork for the background check. Then Gus gave me an oral exam—

"I gotta ask you four questions, it's the law." I could tell he was dreading it. "Have you ever been convicted of a felony?"

"No."

"Have you ever been admitted to a mental health facility as a danger to yourself or others?"

I didn't know how thoroughly they checked, so I was scrupulously honest. "Not exactly." His face began to swell as I explained my uncertainty. "I had a bad acid trip and spent four hours in a psych ward until I came down. I was only nineteen. I'd been to a Buffalo Springfield concert and I couldn't stop dancing."

Gus wheezed impatiently. "Were you a danger to anyone?"

"If anything I was overly amorous. I went home and made love all night. It was my first date with my first husband. The marriage was annulled after a week. I don't even count it."

Gus moved on. "Have you ever been found 'not guilty' by reason of insanity, incompetent to stand trial, or placed under a conservatorship?"

"No." But I couldn't help but wonder, "Do the wackjobs that come in here ever admit to such things? Has anyone ever answered yes?"

"No." Gus asked the final question, "Is there a restraining order against you?"

"No."

"Maybe I'll get one." I smiled politely and told him I'd see him next week. He noted the time, it was three forty-two. "You have to wait a full ten days, to the hour, to the minute."

"I don't even believe in guns, but I can't deny being excited." Gus pressed the buzzer that opens the door and told me to go.

The next day I went to Norman Kaufman's house to look around. The footsteps I heard when I shot the sex tape were probably related to the ransacking, which was probably related to the murder. Doyle said that it's good to go back to the scene of the crime. It might jog my memory or reveal a new clue. Norman's house was for sale. According to Limber, who was a real estate agent, it was a foreclosure. Limber got me in the house, posing as a potential buyer. He had another showing, so he had to leave. "If you find any dead bodies, don't mention my name."

It was getting dark, so I started with the backyard. I stood outside the bedroom window where I shot the sex tape and tried to see where the footsteps might have come from. It could have been the driveway, or the hillside that butted up against the property. I decided to climb the hill and see for myself. I was wearing my Saucony Jazz running shoes. I never run in them, the bouncing up and down is horrible for an aging face. But I walk in them constantly, I wear them all day. I can have those suckers on for twelve hours and not even be aware of my feet.

I hiked to the top of the hill. Kip and Amanda's house was on the other side. I could also see Franky's house from where I stood. The Oscar used to bludgeon Mike was found on this hill. Whoever killed him had escaped this way.

I went back inside the house. The living room was nearly bare. I remembered Mike's body lying on the floor, and a chill ran through me. I went to the master bedroom where he had been very much alive, having hot sex with Jessica. I got another chill. Death and sex had the same effect. I had to pee, so I went into the bathroom. I stared at myself in the mirror. Vanity is my way of avoiding feelings.

I heard a noise coming from the bedroom. I spun around and armed myself with the toilet tank lid. I started out of the bathroom and collided with Norman, who was armed with a wooden hanger. We both screamed and struck each other with our improvised weapons. Norman stumbled to the bed and began to hyperventilate. I dumped out a pillow and told him to breathe into the pillow case.

I explained I was a private detective investigating Mike's murder, and Norman started to calm down. I remained cautious. "I thought you were on location in Vegas."

Norman sniveled into the pillow case. "I got fired. The bank owns my house, I have nowhere to go, no career, no money, no Mike to fix it. All I had going for me was being a director, I'll never get laid again. I won an Oscar, but I don't know what I did right so I can't repeat it, and now it's a murder weapon. It's Kafkaesque. I never read Kafka, I'm full of shit."

I stood up and he grabbed my hand. "Please don't leave me." I was afraid he might off himself, and I loved his one good movie. So I took Norman home with me.

I called Margo. "You have a new client." She met us at the loft and started spinning Norman a new story. He was not fired, he quit because the studio was turning his taut thriller into action drivel. His house was not in foreclosure, he was selling because his best friend had been murdered there. And there was no truth to the rumor he was doing a remake of *Chinatown*. "There's no better way to start a rumor than to deny it," Margo told Norman, who was curled up on my couch.

While Margo worked the phones, I worked my Cuisinart. Emma's party was the next night. I used to spend days prepping Thanksgiving dinner, but with the ransacking and a murder to solve, who had time to obsess over place settings or some novel ingredient to complicate the stuffing? I'd get food on my industrial-sized table and hope for the best. It's the people that matter, it always was.

Watson assisted me in the kitchen. I put Norman to work chopping onions, it gave him cover so he could cry. Hacker smelled cooking, so he came over. He picked the corn bread out of the stuffing as he sliced the green beans. "I like being a dick's bitch."

Norman dried his eyes. "I do too."

Watson stopped chopping. "This bitch is done." Margo and Watson headed out together. My two best friends couldn't be less alike. Watson caught my smile. "Miss Dick thinks she's cool with her ebony and ivory homies." It's true, I do.

I rubbed Kosher salt inside and outside the turkey and stuck it in a plastic bag overnight so it would be juicy. Hacker went home. Norman crashed on my couch. I was up at dawn, baking a pumpkin pie and a birthday cake. Then I wrapped Emma's gift using the yellow crime-scene tape instead of ribbon.

Norman talks in his sleep. I listened to him direct a movie while

I worked. "Let's do a two-shot, just me and Mike. Action . . . Hit him on the head. Now see the blood. Don't worry about an alibi, we'll fix it in post." Norman started to whimper and I started to worry. My houseguest was still a suspect.

My door buzzed and Norman woke up. "Good morning," I said cautiously.

"I dreamt I killed Mike," Norman confessed. The real killer would never admit that. Unless he knew he talked in his sleep. I didn't know what to think.

The door buzzed again. I heard Stella doing Brando as Stanley Kowalski in *Streetcar*. "It's Stelllaaa . . . Stelllaaa . . . "

I ran to the door. "You made it!" Stella was a one-man party, a guaranteed good time.

"I wouldn't miss my cousin's birthday and the sacrificial bird." He applauded my stenciled Private Detective door. "I love what you've done with the place."

Norman stared at Stella who travels as J.Lo, big-hair wig and low-cut dress. Stella gushed, "Mr. Kaufman, I'm a huge fan." He shook Norman's hand. "Stella Sontag. I auditioned for you once. You probably don't remember me, I was playing a man."

"Stella," Norman said in a parched falsetto. He had fallen through the looking glass and landed on my couch. I sent them to the market to buy some stuff that I forgot. By the time they came back, they had adjusted to each other. Norman was just an out-of-work director and Stella was just another tranny. They whipped yams while reciting dialogue from favorite movies. My Thanksgiving elves had found common ground.

The guests started to arrive. Hacker brought me one of his laptops to replace the one that was stolen. "Happy Thanksgiving." I promised him the best of the bird and all the stuffing he could eat.

Margo went straight for the bar. George was in Cape Cod meeting Limber's family, and she wasn't invited. "Bringing your gay lover's ex-wife to Thanksgiving dinner is frowned upon." She poured a glass of the 1985 Chateau Margaux she brought in honor of Emma's birth and got sotted.

Emma didn't invite any of her friends because her age was a

secret. Everyone thought she was twenty-six, including her married boyfriend and boss. She was surprised to see Norman at her party. "Will all your suspects be celebrating my birthday?" she asked her mother.

As his publicist, Margo chimed in. "Norman doesn't have the balls to kill anyone."

Watson was in charge of my mother. June was all done up in ruffles and rouge for the occasion. They did their Laurel and Hardy routine—

"You eat them nuts and your teeth will come out," Watson warned.

"Because I don't have any Poligrip."

"You're the fool who put it in the freezer."

"I thought the cold would soothe my gums."

Stella went on a cranberry sauce and Poligrip run. As J.Lo. In Ralph's market. Imagine the story other shoppers told at their Thanksgiving tables.

Gary arrived with a gift for Emma and the annual porcelain turkey for me. We were no longer a married couple, we were a couple of parents who loved their kid. I hugged him for old time's sake and put the thirtieth turkey in the menagerie.

Candy brought me a lopsided cherry pie. "It tastes better than it looks," she said in her Alabama Monroe. Any fondness I felt for Gary was obliterated by his ogling eye. Candy saw Norman and breathlessly effused, "Oh my god, it's Norman Kaufman." She turned to me. "He's on my list!"

Norman went from Kafkaesque to born-again Hollywood. "I hope you're an actress, that face belongs in front of a camera." Directors go for goddesses and goddesses go for them.

I was surprised Doyle accepted my invitation. This was his first outing since the stroke. His paralyzed mouth and the limp made him reluctant to be around people. "Your people don't matter, it'll be good practice." He had a glass of Margo's Margaux and studied the murder board.

My family and friends sat around the oversized table overeating. Gary told the story of Emma's birth. She was born on Thanksgiving Day, two weeks ahead of schedule. We were at

Ronald's house having dinner, most of the guests were doctors and their wives. I sat next to Stella, who was nine at the time and still known as Stanley. I was reaching for the gravy when my water broke. Stanley was a bed wetter and seeing an adult wet herself triggered some sympathetic mechanism, his water broke too. I stood up and lost my balance. I grabbed the lace tablecloth as I fell, bringing down the dinner, including the turkey. I lay on the floor, having a contraction, covered in Thanksgiving. One of the doctors was a gynecologist. He stuck his hand up my skirt and pronounced me four centimeters dilated. I never really liked this guy, and now he was fingering my who-ha in front of my husband.

Gary tells the story much better than me. He always ends it by saying, "We got to the hospital, and Emma emerged giving us much to be thankful for."

Normally, Emma adores that story, but this time she was upset. "I peaked at birth. I'm thirty years old and what have I done with my life?"

"You are not thirty," my mother insisted.

"I didn't find my calling until I was sixty-seven," I said to Emma.

"You are not sixty-seven," my mother insisted.

Emma wailed, "I have no husband, I hate my job. I make reality TV—my calling is to find the next *Duck Dynasty*."

Margo wallowed. "Having no husband is better than one that leaves you for another man."

Candy despaired in her breathy Southern drawl, "I was raised in a 'Duck Dynasty.'"

Stella lamented, "At least you weren't beaten up for wearing a dress."

A drunken Doyle slurred, "At least you didn't have a stroke."

June would not be outdone. "You are not the only one limping, sir, my gout is so bad I had to wear slippers." She lifted a veiny leg and displayed her slipper. "Every inch of me is infirm. A stroke," she said dismissively, "I have a medical crisis every month."

"And I gotta take her infirm ass to some fuckinologist," Watson said as she cut June's meat.

Margo raised her glass. "Let's all be bloody unthankful. It's more honest than the traditional gratitudes. Pilgrims broke bread with some Indians, and we're supposed to bullshit our way through another meal." Everyone drank to that. "What are you unthankful for, Billie?"

I was having so much fun I had to think for a minute. "I'm unthankful I haven't solved my case."

Norman looked at the murder board. "I'm unthankful I'm a suspect."

Margo didn't like Norman's picture. "We have to get you a better headshot."

Doyle tried to pump Norman. "If you didn't do it, who did?"

"I bet it was Amanda's ugly husband." My mother squinted at the murder board. "What's his name again?"

"My money is still on Whitey," Watson said.

Hacker threw a dollar on the table. "Let's start a pool. I think it was Rusty."

Gary threw down a dollar. "My money is on the first wife."

"Sarah didn't do it," I said with certainty.

Doyle pulled rank. "A phony confession to protect her son doesn't mean she didn't do it. Maybe it was a double twist, a very clever way to exonerate herself."

Stella anted up. "I think it was the son. I totally get killing your father."

Norman tossed in a dollar. "From *The Maltese Falcon* to *Presumed Innocent,* it's Film School 101. The killer is always a denouement shocker. I think it was Felicia."

Doyle was intrigued. "She didn't have an alibi."

Margo argued, "If Felicia did it, why would she hire a private detective?"

"It wouldn't be the first time the guilty party used that cover," Doyle said. "And she didn't hire an experienced pro. She knew Billie would never figure it out."

My rehiring had always been suspicious, but I was not about to bet against myself. "It can't be Felicia, who's going to pay me?"

Candy threw in a dollar and said breathlessly, "I think it was Mike's assistant, Pam. She was so weird at the gallery. She asked if my breasts were real. I said, 'Absolutely.'" All the men at the table were staring at Candy's chest. "Then she asked if I ever slept with Mike, and I said I never even met him. She called me a liar and squeezed my boob. Since I lied about my implants, she thought I was lying about Mike and called me a slut."

Margo polished off the Margaux and placed her bet. "I think it was Billie. She was at the scene of the crime and she had the hots for the victim."

Doyle slurred, "Billie had the hots for Mike?"

Watson piled on. "All this dicking around was just to cover her tracks."

I dug out an 8×10 glossy from my acting days and stuck it on the murder board. "This is a masturbatory investigation." I threw in a dollar. "I think I did it."

It was my favorite Thanksgiving Birthday ever. Emma cut the cake and the pumpkin pie. She opened my gift—a Vera Wang trench coat in lieu of a wedding dress. She tied the yellow crime-scene tape in a bow around her neck and gave me the longest hug of her adult life. My kid liked me, at least she liked me that night.

I plucked dollar bills off the table and stuck them in my cleavage. My guests begged me not to strip and I obliged. My picture stayed on the murder board. With three bets, I was the prime suspect.

20
VIDEO FOLLIES

Murder or no murder, I went shopping on Black Friday. I was not one of those fanatics that hits the stores at midnight. I waited until 5 a.m. Coupons are a siren song to a mall warrior in need of towels, and a sweater to go with the pants that would fit me in five pounds, and the suede ankle booties that didn't go with anything but made me feel hip. My real talent is returning. I once got Macy's to take back a skirt I bought at Robinsons two years after they went out of business. Macy's bought them out, and so they were responsible for the defective zipper. I exhausted the salesgirl and the manager, who gave me a store credit which I used to buy the pants that would fit me in five pounds.

It was Black Friday night. I ate fried stuffing and pondered the murder board in the Calvin Klein sweats I got at half price. The phone rang. It was Felicia. Someone sent her the sex tape of Mike and Jessica. I jumped in my car and got to Brentwood as fast as I could.

In between bouts of outrage and tears, she told me what happened. A man left a package on her doorstep. He rang the bell and took off before the housekeeper saw him. Felicia opened the package and inside was the DVD. There was a short note—"Watch this and wait for my call." Felicia watched the video, then the man called and said he wanted a hundred thousand dollars to keep the X-rated sex tape off the Internet.

"I have to pay him. My father would be horrified if this got out. And my baby, this is not how I want him to think of Mike. If it's on the Internet, it will never go away."

"The blackmailing will never end," I said solemnly. "I'm pretty sure I know who it is. Mike was being blackmailed by Jessica's boyfriend, Rusty. He threatened to tell you about Mike's affair with Jessica." Felicia was glad Mike loved her enough to preserve their marriage, that meant more than the extortion. I tried to tell her how desperate Rusty was. "He's a junkie, no amount of money will ever be enough."

"When did he shoot that video? Did Jessica know, do you think she was in on it?"

My gut was churning with guilt. I had to tell her the truth. "Rusty didn't shoot it."

"How do you know that?"

"I shot it. When I was following Mike."

Felicia's back stiffened, she was ice-cold. "Why didn't you show it to me? That's why I hired you. I wanted to know if my husband was sleeping with other women."

"I told about you about the affairs. But I didn't think you needed to see him in action. You were pregnant. I was trying to protect you."

"How did this Rusty get a copy?"

"My loft was ransacked. A lot of stuff was stolen, I didn't even realize the DVD was missing at first. I still can't be sure it was Rusty. Give me a chance to find out and make this right. Don't pay him, not yet."

"He said he'd put it on the Internet."

"Then he'd have nothing to blackmail you with. Stall him. Tell him your money is tied up in a trust that your father controls, and you'll need a few days to get it."

Felicia was lost in a dark thought. "My father said Mike had been taking money out of their offshore accounts. I didn't believe him."

I learned a valuable lesson. Just because you don't like a guy, it doesn't mean he did the crime. It was likeable Mike who was stealing from Whitey to pay Rusty the blackmail money. Plus the townhouse and the Mercedes that Whitey unwittingly bought his son-in-law's mistress. What tangled webs men weave with their johnsons.

Felicia agreed to give me some time. I went straight to Doyle. We tried to figure out our next move. The footsteps I heard when I shot the sex tape had to belong to Rusty. He was jealous, he was following Jessica, and there I was making my little porno. He was the ransacker and the blackmailer. But was he the killer?

We wasted a day staking out Rusty's house, he never showed. No drug deals in The Velvet Swing parking lot. The cell phone that Hacker tapped was dead. Doyle suggested I pay Jessica a visit. Maybe Rusty had been in touch in with her, and we could get a lead on him.

I went to see Jessica in her swanky townhouse. As I walked up to the front door, it occurred to me that Rusty could be inside holding her hostage. I hid in the bushes trying to assess the situation. Standing in the mud, I had a deja vu. My career began in the bushes outside Gary's office. It felt like a lifetime ago, but it had only been three months.

I heard the TV and peeked in Jessica's living room window. I saw no sign of Rusty, just the blond hair and the long legs stretched out on the couch. She was watching a *Jersey Shore* rerun. I don't care how long the legs, how could Mike be so taken with this girl? I went to the door and rang the bell.

An older version of Jessica opened the door. The hair was blond but thinning. The face was buried under makeup that caked in the creases. The showgirl body was sagging. But it's the eyes I'll never forget. You know crazy when you see it. Intense but unfocused. Afraid and yet frightening.

"May I help you?" she asked too eagerly.

"I'm looking for Jessica." The door opened wider and she let me in.

"I'm her mother, Gloria. Jessie should be home any minute."

Gloria turned off the TV and offered me some of her rice crispy treats. She ignored the crumbs sticking to her angora sweater as we chatted. Gloria had been in a mental-health facility. She was very frank about it, proud even. Spending Thanksgiving outside the bin was a milestone.

I asked if she'd ever met Rusty. Gloria pursed her lips. "Jessie was only seventeen. Jailbait. He saw her in the mall and said he could make her a star. He took lots of pictures and sent them to magazines. Next thing you know they move to Hollywood, and I don't see her anymore, excepting in those magazines. With no clothes on. Like mother like daughter."

She stood up and posed, showing off her body. "I was a topless dancer. That's how I met Jessie's daddy. He came in the club and swept me off my feet with a fifty-dollar tip." She sat down and picked rice kernels off her sweater. "He was married. The big tippers usually are. He already had three kids and didn't want anymore. Jessie was the cutest little thing, but not cute enough. He'd bounce her on his knee and bring her toys, then he just faded away."

Gloria winked at me. I wanted to win her over so I winked back. She winked again, I did too. I realized her wink was involuntary. She stared at the blank TV and told me how much the world had changed since she was last in it.

I tried to get her to focus. "Has Rusty been around recently?"

"Jessie broke up with that loser when somebody better came along."

"Are you talking about Mike Armstrong?"

"That's right." She stopped winking. "How did you say you knew Jessie again?"

"I'm trying to help her, Gloria. It's very important I find Rusty. I'm a private detective."

"Really and truly? You don't look the type."

"Really and truly," I assured her. "Did you ever meet Mike?"

"Jessie was afraid I'd scare him off. He was older. And married. I tried to warn her, but she wouldn't listen. He threw all that money at Jessie and then dumped her because his wife was having a baby. I told her not to date a married man. Doesn't matter now. Mike is dead." She smiled like a naughty child, a middle-aged bad seed. "Is that why you're looking for Rusty?"

The front door opened and Jessica walked in. I stood up and introduced myself. "I'm Billie Ridley. I'm trying to find Rusty Savage—"

"She's a private detective," Gloria said.

Jessica looked alarmed. "I have no idea where Rusty is."

Gloria added, "Whenever he calls, Jessie tells him to get lost."

"So you do hear from him," I said to Jessica.

"I'm afraid so. Look, I'm sorry, I have an audition. I have to study my lines."

She was trying to blow me off. I had to give her a reason to help me. "There's something you need to know. Rusty has a sex tape of you and Mike that he's threatening to put on the Internet."

The color drained from Jessica's beautiful face. "Oh, my God."

Gloria had a different take. "It could make you famous." Jessica glared at her mother. "It didn't do Paris Hilton any harm or that *Twilight* girl."

"Kristen Stewart never made a sex tape."

"Well, maybe she should. She's not going to look that good forever. And neither are you."

Jessica turned her back on her mother and looked at me. "When did Rusty make the tape?"

"He didn't make it," I said guardedly.

"Then who did?"

"I'm afraid I can't tell you that."

"Can't or won't?" Jessica was enraged. "Was it Mike? Did he secretly tape us having sex?"

"I told you not to date a married man," Gloria said to her daughter's back.

Jessica spun around. "Will you please shut up?!"

Gloria let her bad seed sprout. "He gave you a Mercedes Benz and a pretty little house to spread your legs in, but he didn't give you his name."

Jessica shot back, "All you got was a fifty-dollar tip."

"And an ungrateful brat that ruined my body. Nobody paid to see my titties after you came along."

Suddenly my mother didn't seem so bad. She was a pain in the ass but she was benign. And underneath all that rouge I knew she

160

loved me. These two were out of an Albee play. Nothing was too cruel, they bantered for blood.

"I'm sorry, my mother's not well," Jessica said as she ushered me out.

"Like mother like daughter!" Gloria yelled.

Jessica walked me to my car. "She was in an institution, but they lost their funding and closed down." She looked back at the house. Gloria was standing in the window. "It's so sad. I want to help her, but I don't know how much more I can take." I gave Jessica my card, and she promised to call me if she heard from Rusty.

I was trying to make sense of what I learned. Gloria was crazy, who knew how much of her story to believe. I updated Doyle. Then I went to see Krasny to put it in context.

When I arrived at his office, Krasny was wearing a patch over one eye. "Are you okay?" I asked apprehensively.

"Cataract surgery." A meaningful pause. "What's wrong, Billie?"

I threw him an insight so we could talk about my case. "I'm afraid of losing you."

"Why so efficient?" Even with one eye, the guy could see right through me.

"I'm trying to avoid my feelings. Can we move on?" I told him about Jessica and her mother. "According to Gloria, Jessica's father was a married man with three kids. He already had a family, so he abandoned Jessica. And so did Mike, who dumped Jessica for his pregnant wife. That must have made her very angry—angry enough to kill him. Maybe that last rendezvous is when he tried to break it off." I shot down my own theory. "Gloria just got out of the bin, maybe she's delusional. She was like an evil little girl, so vindictive, she's jealous of Jessica."

"Can we talk about you instead of your suspects?"

"Okay. I'm jealous of Jessica too. The beautiful blonde who gets all the men. I want her to be the killer. Or maybe I just identify with her father stuff. Gloria knew I was a private detective, maybe she was trying to nail her own daughter for murder." Krasny kept his wise eye on me. I demanded an opinion. "Do you think Jessica did it?"

"What's more important is that you think she did. A daughter is abandoned, and you assume she is angry enough to murder a surrogate."

I was getting angry at my surrogate. "I'm paying for your expertise."

"Solve murders on your own time. The only mystery I'm trying to solve is you."

Then he informs me he will be taking a few weeks off over the holidays. Presumably he will be with his wife and kids who don't have to pay for his company. I wanted to cancel the check I just wrote him—I would be buying his dinner with Alma or the gift he'd give his daughter. But he gave me his wisdom. He knew me. And liked me. I felt an overwhelming affection for Krasny. My emotions can turn on a dime, or two hundred dollars. "Have a good time," was all that came out.

Krasny smiled. "I'll see you next month."

I got home and went straight to the murder board. Watson looked on as I made notes. The white board turned grey from all the erasing. I didn't know if I could trust Gloria's information, or trust myself, you follow the leads you want to believe. "Did Jessica murder Mike?" was the last thing I wrote.

Watson had her doubts. "She's the one that found the body."

"Jessica could have killed him and gone out the back, then returned to discover the body. She paused to primp, making sure people saw her, including a gullible private detective who was taking her time-stamped picture."

"If I kill somebody, I'm gonna use that."

"If it was Jessica, how do I prove it? The police haven't found anything to implicate her. She may get away with it."

Norman shuffled in the door wearing a Hugo Boss suit that didn't fit him. "Margo took me to the Polo Lounge where I denied that Charlize was doing *Chinatown*. He flopped on the couch and looked at the murder board. "You think Jessica killed Mike?"

"Did you know her?" I asked.

"Other than her having sex in my bed, not very well." Norman thought in terms of types. "She's a classic Hitchcock blonde. Cinematically, she would be a great choice."

162

"Jessica gives me a *Basic Instinct* vibe." Talking about movies gave me an idea, the kind that comes once in a dick's career. "If I can make one video, I can make another one."

"That first video got you in a world of trouble," Watson said.

"But the sequel could solve the case." I shared my vision. "We go to Norman's house and recreate the murder. We use a video camera that's a little out of focus as if I were shooting it from outside the living room window, with no sound. Candy can play Jessica. Hacker can play Mike, they're the same height. We only see them from far away, in low light, and very briefly. Then we deliver a copy of the video to Jessica. If she killed him, she'll think it's real."

Norman got it. "I Know What You Did Last Month."

"But you didn't shoot a video that night," Watson said, "you only took those stills."

"Jessica doesn't know that. But she knows there's a sex tape. Another video is not that hard to believe." My pitch went on for another hour, eventually I got a green light.

Doyle thought it was a dumb idea, but he didn't have a better one, so he signed on as technical adviser. Based on the police report and crime-scene photos, we knew how to position the actors to reenact the lethal blow.

Watson handled wardrobe. I sent her to Bloomingdale's, but we left the tags on so everything could be returned. We used the stills I took of Jessica to duplicate her outfit for Candy, and the photos of Mike's body to get a jacket and pants for Hacker. Watson also did props. We needed an Oscar. The police still had Norman's, so she picked one up at a pawn shop. It was a fake, but you couldn't tell from a distance.

I curled Hacker's spiked hair and put some grey at the temples. Candy did her own makeup and we added extensions to get Jessica's hair. They put on their costumes and came to the set. Candy was nervous, she wanted to impress Norman.

"I need to understand my character," Candy said in her Southern Monroe. It's a good thing we didn't have sound. "I've never played a killer before, usually I'm the victim. What would drive her to do such a thing?"

"Mike was leaving her," I said helpfully. That wasn't enough, so I gave her Jessica's backstory. "An absent father, a crazy mother, very crazy, she was in an institution."

Candy gasped. "That's Marilyn's backstory. No one knows for sure who her father was. And her mother, Gladys, was in an institution most of Marilyn's life."

Another Gladys. Same as Elvis Presley's mother. Same as my father's girlfriend. Maybe Murray was dating Marilyn's mother.

Norman did some blocking to correspond with the crime-scene photos. Doyle showed Candy how to hit Hacker with the Oscar based on the direction of the blood splatter.

"Maybe we should kiss before she whacks me," Hacker suggested

"No lipstick traces were found on the corpse," Doyle advised.

"Just to get in character, we don't have to film it," Hacker said to his leading lady.

Norman pounded his chest. "I am the director." There would be no kiss. Instead he had them improvise a fight. Hacker was too gentle, so Norman started provoking Candy. "No wonder he dumped you, you can't act."

"You can't direct!" Candy raged breathlessly.

"Let's do a take." Norman went outside and shot them through the window. Candy picked up the Oscar and hit Hacker. She barely grazed him, but he went down as rehearsed.

Doyle said we had to do it again. Hacker landed in the wrong position. We did a few more takes . . . Candy dropped the Oscar, Hacker touched her breast before she hit him. But the fourth take was great. You couldn't see Candy's face, but the body language was perfect, and Hacker fell just right.

"That's a wrap!" Norman declared after viewing the footage.

"Can I get a copy for my reel?" Candy asked.

Norman offered her a part in his next movie, if he ever worked again, which he seriously doubted. Candy interrupted his downward spiral with an invitation to crash at her place. My heart went out to Hacker, but neo-geek neighbors were not on her list.

Norman and I edited the video. "Make it more grainy . . . lose focus when she turns around . . . I love how the light hits the Oscar right before it comes down." When we were done, you'd swear you were watching the real thing. But would it play as well with Jessica?

I delivered the video the same way that Rusty delivered the sex tape to Felicia. I put it on Jessica's doorstep, rang the bell and took off. She opened the door, picked up the package and went back inside. The note was simple—"I know what you did. Meet me at Jolly's restaurant in Hollywood at midnight."

Jolly's was Doyle's idea. He wanted somewhere very public to minimize the danger. He often confronted bad guys at Jolly's and knew the territory. It started out as a family restaurant and changed with the neighborhood. The midnight crowd included rowdy kids looking for a cheap burger, hookers, stoners drifting in from nearby clubs.

I sat in a booth. I was wearing a wire perched between my breasts. Doyle sat at a booth across from mine. He had a hidden video camera. And he was packing heat, just in case.

Cora, the waitress, came over with menus. She was a '50s throwback with a nametag on her uniform. "What'll it be?" she asked Doyle.

"Just coffee, honey."

I looked at the menu, but I was too nervous to eat. "I'll just have green tea."

"We only got regular," Cora said as she walked off.

At the stroke of midnight my eyes were glued to the door. Ten minutes, fifteen minutes passed. I was going nuts. I ordered some food to sustain myself. "I'll have the green salad with the dressing on the side. Just oil and vinegar, but only if it's olive oil."

"Olive oil, on the side," Cora said in a deadpan and walked off.

Doyle glared at me. I defended my choice. "Most oils have omega-6s—corn oil, soybean oil—which is bad for the heart and the brain." I was trying to reach Doyle's brain so I put it in terms that might resonate. "In countries where they eat lots of omega-6 oils and not enough omega-3s, the murder rate is twenty times higher, that's how much they screw you up."

"Maybe Jessica had too much omega-6 and that's why she killed Mike, why don't you ask her about that?"

I finished my salad. Still no Jessica. With every passing minute, I grew more anxious. I ordered some carbs to calm myself down. "Do you have any sweet potatoes?" Cora nodded no. "Brown rice?' Her deadpan stare suggested they did not. I looked at the menu. "I'll have some pasta . . . al dente."

"We don't serve pasta al dante."

I pulled a Jack Nicholson in *Five Easy Pieces* when he tangled with a hostile waitress. "You have spaghetti and meatballs." I pointed to the picture in the plastic menu.

"Yeah," Cora said with deadpan contempt.

"Give me the spaghetti and meatballs." Cora wrote down my order. "Now hold the meatballs and give me parmesan cheese instead. And don't overcook it."

"It's already cooked, they make it in the morning with the meatballs mixed in. You can pick them out if you want."

"Just give me some hash browns," I said. Cora walked off smirking.

When I finished my hash browns, Doyle called the operation off. "Jessica's not coming."

"Let's give it another ten minutes." I ordered more food to buy time and steady my nerves. I was on my second rice pudding when a well-built blonde walked in. I put down my spoon and braced myself. As she grew nearer, I could see it wasn't Jessica. The clubs were closing, and a new wave of customers started to arrive. Blonde after blonde walked in, short ones, tall ones, none of them were Jessica. At three o'clock I gave up. I paid the bill and woke Doyle.

"She's not coming," I conceded. Doyle left Cora a twenty-dollar apology for bringing me in.

"I told you it was a dumb idea," Doyle said when I dropped him off. I watched him limping away. His omega-6 brain took one more shot. "You're a lousy date."

I drove past Jessica's place on my way home. Her Mercedes was parked in the driveway. The lights were off inside the house. My dumb idea began to plague me. Jessica knew the video was fake because she didn't kill Mike. What if she took it to the cops, I could get busted for extortion. I'd never get my license. I could go to jail.

I was up all night revising the murder board in desperate search of a theory. There was only one thing I knew for certain—I didn't know what the fuck I was doing.

21
BANG

When Watson arrived the next day, I still hadn't been to sleep. The murder board was covered in question marks and possibilities. Watson eased the marking pen out of my hand. "You best give it a rest, your eyes are bugging outta your head."

"Time is running out," I protested.

"Mike will still be dead tomorrow. You can figure out who done it then."

"Felicia will have to pay Rusty all that money. I didn't help my client, I hurt her." My bloodshot eyes landed on the Oscar we used in the video. I stuck it in my turkey menagerie as a symbol of my absurdity. "A sixty-seven-year-old dick, what was I thinking?"

Watson made me a green drink and then took my mother to physical therapy. I started to nod off when Doyle called. I sounded so down he was nice to me. "Cheer up, Ridley. In six thousand hours you'll be pretty good at this."

I went back to the murder board and filled it with weak theories. When I looked up it was almost three. I threw on some clothes and headed for Gun City. My ten-day waiting period had ended.

Gus buzzed me in the door. "You're early," he said with some misgiving. I looked as rotten as I felt. "You seem a little weird, even for you. Have you been drinking?"

"Carrot juice and kale," I said bitterly. "Can I have my gun?"

He looked at the clock. "In seventeen minutes. The law says you gotta wait exactly ten days, to the minute. You'll get your gun at three forty-two."

"Like waiting those seventeen minutes will keep me from shooting someone I shouldn't." Gus had another customer, so I took a seat and nodded off. Seventeen minutes later, he woke me up and gave me my pearl-handled .38. "Can I return it if I don't like owning a gun?" Gus pressed the buzzer and told me never to come back.

"Billie got her gun" kept repeating inside my head as I drove through the heavy traffic. I used to tool around LA at a reasonable speed, now it has the worst traffic in the nation. I secretly wished for an earthquake, just strong enough to get the shaken to relocate. "Billie got her gun, Billie got her gun." I found myself driving up Laurel Canyon to Rusty's house. I parked down the street and began my vigil. When I woke up it was dark. I fell asleep on a stakeout, that's what us elderly dicks do. I gave up and headed home. "Billie got her gun, Billie got her gun."

When all else fails, get sick. I had a sore throat, a stuffy nose, I even managed a headache. An excuse to get under the covers and hide from my life.

Candy came by with Norman and Hacker and an invitation to a screening of her edgy Daisy Duke movie. I sneezed and declined, citing my poor health. I apologized for involving them in my video follies, but no one seemed to mind. They wished me a speedy recovery and offered to bring back chicken soup.

I knew I had to call Felicia but couldn't bring myself to do it. My head was pounding, I was acutely congested, so I allowed myself to wait until morning.

Billie got her gun but didn't know where to keep it. I hid it in Stella's closet, inside his Elizabeth Taylor turban. I moved it to my sock drawer for easier access. If I needed it, I would need it fast. I couldn't tell an intruder to wait while I go get my gun. Which is how it ended up on my nightstand, next to the vanilla and the body lotion I make out of shea butter and coconut oil. It's greasy but very effective.

I went to the kitchen and prepared Dr. Weil's infection-fighting remedy. It works on everything from candida to a cold. A large clove of raw garlic squeezed through a garlic press. Let it sit out for ten minutes to oxidize. Then swallow it down, followed by a glass of water so it doesn't burn. Any bugs lurking in any body part will run for another body.

I had the heat on which made the air too dry, so I made it moist. Next to my scale, my humidifier is my favorite device. Warm mist is best in winter because it heats the room and cuts down on the utility bill. But above all else, it's great for the skin.

I put Scotch tape on my eleven lines and climbed into bed. I slathered body lotion on my hands and feet. The gun was pointing at my pillow. I picked it up to turn it around and got shea butter on my gun. I stared at the items on my nightstand—vanilla to calm myself, lotion to hydrate my aging extremities, and a greasy gun. That pretty much described me.

Beep beep, blink blink, I finally fell asleep. I often dreamt about my case and this night was no exception. Logan was at my place conducting a lineup of all the suspects. They stood in front of the murder board, and I had to decide which one killed Mike. I walked up and down looking deep into their souls. "I still think Jessica did it." But Jessica wasn't in the lineup. She was outside my glass door. Billie Ridley Private Detective shattered into a million pieces as she broke into the loft.

I woke up. There was broken glass on the floor. Jessica was racing toward me, holding a gun. *This was no dream—this was real!*

I groped for my greasy gun, but it slid off the nightstand. I jumped out of bed and my legs buckled. I knelt before Jessica, trying to sound tough. "Killing me won't do any good." I was nose-to-nose with the 9mm Glock pistol she held in her hand. It was too masculine for Jessica, especially with the white gloves she was wearing.

"Stand up!"

I got to my feet. "You're not angry at me, this is mother stuff. I don't blame you, I met your mother."

"Shut your mouth!" Jessica shrieked.

I tried to stall. Anything to stay alive. "Why did you murder Mike? Was he going to leave you? Men can be such assholes, my husband left me for an infomercial model and she wasn't even pregnant."

Her furious eyes stared above mine. "Why do you have tape on your forehead?"

"To smooth out my eleven lines."

"A private detective," Jessica hissed, "how old are you anyway?"

"Sixty-seven."

"You crazy old lady. I would have gotten away with it. Now I have to kill you!"

I couldn't breathe. She didn't need to shoot me, I was having a heart attack. "Goodbye Billie," I cried inside. I would miss me. I closed my eyes and prepared to die.

Then I opened them again. I heard footsteps in the hall. I thought it might be Hacker with my chicken soup and tried to warn him. "Look out, Jessica has a gun!"

"My gun!" Rusty roared as he walked through the shattered door. He was coked up and out for blood.

Jessica freaked out. "How did you find me?!"

"I followed you!" Rusty grabbed me by the hair and screamed at Jessica. "You shoot this bitch with my gun and the cops will think I did it because she knew I killed Mike." He turned my terrified face toward his. "Jessica killed Mike, she's setting me up!"

"I know," I said in a choked whisper.

Rusty let go of me and raged at Jessica, "I'm not gonna hang for you!"

"You're right, Rusty, that was the plan." Jessica picked up my gun, which was under the nightstand. "But this is better." She held a gun in each of her gloved hands. Jessica pointed Rusty's pistol at me—"You shot Billie." She pointed my revolver at Rusty—"And Billie shot you." Jessica smiled, she looked like her mother.

"Thanks for stopping by," she said to Rusty as she pulled the trigger. My gun was so greasy, she missed his gut and hit him in the groin.

Rusty lunged at Jessica. "I'll kill you!" Jessica shot him again. I didn't wait to see who won. I threw open the window and hurled myself onto the fire escape. I twisted my ankle so badly I could barely stand. The adrenaline kicked in, and I hobbled down the metal ladder and jumped to the ground.

Jessica was right behind me. I ran into the street, trying to get to the Bada Bang. She shot at me, but I kept on running. Jessica followed me into the street. I heard a car as it hit the brakes. I turned around—it was Mike's Porsche. The top was down, music was blaring, there was a painting of Candy in the back seat. Danny was at the wheel. He hit Jessica so hard her body went flying to the curb. The Porsche came to a screeching stop.

Danny cried, "Nooo, nooo, please, no . . . "

Jessica was lying in the gutter. I got down and leaned over her body to see if she was still alive. She grabbed me and said with her last breath, "I'm scared."

The beautiful blonde who got all the men died in my arms. Try getting over that.

Customers came out of the bar. Tony had his baseball bat. Someone called 911. Danny was crying so hard he could barely hear me. "She killed your father and she was going to kill me." I made him look at me. "You saved my life."

Danny looked at Jessica and saw the gun in her hand. He rocked back and forth. "Okay, okay, okay," he repeated as he began to understand.

I heard sirens. Time stood still. I don't know when the police arrived. I was numb by then, or in shock. There was a medic taking care of Danny. They put Rusty in an ambulance. The flashing red lights and the Bada Bang's neon sign were blinking in unison. It created an eerie strobe in which to view a death. I was in a B-movie again.

Logan's unmarked car came to an abrupt stop. He pulled up in the same car the night Mike was murdered. Logan meant nothing to me then. On this night, the hardest of my life, he was the second coming. The broad shoulders headed my way. I finally let myself fall apart. He held me in his arms for all to see. The other cops, the press that started to gather. I pulled out of the embrace before anyone knew, including Logan, how hard it was to let him go.

"Thanks, Detective Logan," I said as I withdrew. He smiled. He knew.

The cops awaited his orders and Logan took command. Margo arrived and started working the reporters on my behalf. Logan was asked for a statement. He gave me credit for solving Mike's murder. "Billie Ridley is a first-rate detective."

The first-rate detective dissolved. Margo knew I had a crush, but she had never met him. "That's the guy?" she asked.

"That's the guy," I confirmed.

"Unrequited love is the only kind that lasts."

The drama was over. Everyone was leaving. They carted Jessica off in a body bag. I looked at the chalk drawing that outlined her demise. Who was to blame for her noir ending? Her mother, a missing father, the men like Mike who took advantage of her need, the women like me who envied her? I felt no sense of triumph, only remorse. The perp was also a victim.

I went home. There was yellow crime-scene tape outside my shattered door. Watson and Doyle waited for me to come out of the bathroom. I have no idea how long I was in there. I was washing Jessica's blood off my hands. I scrubbed and scrubbed, trying to rid myself of my torment.

"Out, out damned spot!" I cried.

In high school we did *Macbeth*. I was cast as one of the three witches, but the girl who played Lady Macbeth got mono so I went on. Fifty years later I grew into the role.

"Out damned spot, out I say." I forgot some of the lines, but not the intent. "Who would have thought the blonde to have so much blood in her?"

Watson yelled from the other side of the door, "Who you talking to?"

I rubbed my hands together. "Will these hands ne'er be clean?"

Watson yelled, "There's some Ajax under the sink."

I sniffed my hand. "Here's the smell of the blood still. All the perfumes of Arabia will not sweeten this little hand."

Watson yelled, "Soak your little hand in vanilla."

I came out of the bathroom rubbing my hands. Doyle lost patience with his protege. "Blood on your hands is a rite of passage."

Tears filled my eyes. "What's done cannot be undone."

Doyle bellowed, "Dicks don't cry."

22
NEVER ENDING

The next day, I went to see my client. Now I understood Doyle's loyalty to Mike. The client comes first. I felt fiercely protective of Felicia, I don't even know when that happened. Doyle says it has to be that way, otherwise there is no honor in what we do.

I told Felicia what she wanted to know. "Mike ended the affair with Jessica because you were pregnant. He was trying to do right by you and the child you are carrying. I believe he died in love with his wife."

Felicia's hand came to rest on her belly. "I don't have to be angry anymore. My son will only see the affection for his father in my eyes."

I opened my purse and took out a copy of the sex tape that Rusty was using to blackmail Felicia. "There are no more copies. I went to Rusty's house last night and did some ransacking of my own."

I also recovered my laptop and cameras. After my hand-washing soliloquy, I pulled myself together and headed for Rusty's house. I had to get the tape before the cops found it and it became evidence. It was my maiden B and E. I have to say, I rather enjoyed it.

My client thanked me. She was airbrushed. I was crude. Not her kind of dame but now forever bound. I was grateful for her gratitude, my new drug of choice.

With some reluctance, I erased the murder board. Every detail, every clue was wiped away. I took down all the photographs. But I kept Mike's. I still have it. You never forget your first case.

I started taking better care of myself. Having almost died, I realized how much I wanted to live. I was only sixty-seven and just hitting my stride, I would eat and exercise accordingly. Too bad we don't do right without a bullet or a biopsy to scare us straight.

My stenciled door has bullet-proof glass. Billie Ridley Private Detective is well protected. Watson got a raise. She gets a piece of my action. Margo was turning me into a celebrity sleuth. The novice who solved the high-profile case. Technically, I was still under Doyle's wing, amassing my six thousand hours to get licensed. But I had wings of my own. Women of a certain age wanted a dick they could relate to. The phones were ringing off the hook. My specialty was adultery, and I was in the right town.

One of those calls was from Regina Harrington Tate, a famously wealthy heiress. Margo gave me the gossipy details. Regina was known as the Queen of Pasadena. Her father made his considerable fortune in plastics. Her husband, Montgomery Tate, was an East Coast blue blood whose family fortune was long since blown. He married for money and presumably screwed around.

I was not to come to her palatial home in Pasadena—greater LA's last bastion of old money. She would come to me, in order to keep our meeting secret.

Regina arrived at my loft the next afternoon. She wore a simple black sheath, expensive blond hair, her thin skin wrinkled and pale. She appeared older than her forty-eight years. She looked around disapprovingly as if she entered an unclean area. There was a hesitation before taking a seat. "I rarely come downtown." She glanced at my bed. "Do you like living here?"

"Yes." We were already at an impasse. I pulled a Krasny and let her stew in her own discomfort. She wasn't used to being challenged. My stock went up.

"Felicia Armstrong spoke very highly of you. She cochairs one of my charities."

Good word of mouth is invaluable in my line of work. I hid my pleasure, not wishing to divulge anything about a client, including her relationship with me. I was selling discretion and Regina was buying.

"I've been married to Monty for nine years." A fine layer of perspiration appeared on her brow. She couldn't bring herself to broach the infidelity, so I broke the ice.

"I was married for thirty years, my husband cheated on me throughout the marriage."

Regina bristled. "Is that meant to make me confide in you?"

"Yes." Another impasse.

"I wish my concerns were so mundane." She looked over at Watson, who was sitting at her desk and vaguely in earshot. "I'm not feeling very well, I wonder if I might have a glass of water."

I introduced them. "This is my associate, Watson."

"*Watson,*" Regina repeated incredulously.

"Anything you have to say to me you can say in front of her."

"May I have a glass of water?" was all she had to say.

Watson headed for the kitchen. "Keep your secrets, honey, I take no offense."

Regina lowered her voice. "Our tenth wedding anniversary is approaching. That has enormous financial consequences. If Monty is humiliating me with other women, I would like to know that before he gets any more of my money." I nodded knowingly. Regina scowled. "I don't think you understand. This is a matter of property, not of the heart."

She was desperate and disdainful. And very hard to like. Just as I was doubting I should take her case, Regina took out her checkbook. "Will a ten-thousand-dollar retainer suffice?" It sufficed. I could put up with rude for that kind of money.

Her hand trembled as she gave me the check. "Monty is no fool, he will not be easy to catch. And I will require proof." Her breathing became more labored. I couldn't tell if this was emotion or illness. "I don't want the lurid details of his indiscretions to become public knowledge." Regina was as white as the murder board behind her. "He has very a robust sexual appetite." She was losing consciousness. "And he . . . and he . . . "

Her frightened eyes locked on mine as she fell out of her chair. She was lying facedown on my unclean floor, her skirt hiked above her haunches. The Queen of Pasadena was not wearing underwear.

TO BE CONTINUED...

ACKNOWLEDGMENTS

I am dripping with gratitude to so many people. The initial readers for giving me such great notes: Colleen Palermo, Judith Lutz, Ken Pisani, and Lynne Farr, who gave me invaluable input and *disabused me of my need to italicize*. Amanda Pisani, my wise editor and literary last stop. The panicky phone call advisors: Lynn Tufeld, Anna Mills, Patti and Donald Ross, and Susan Epstein, who also contributed the kale recipe. Self-publishing goddess, Christiana Miller, for generously sharing her vast knowledge. The multitalented Jennifer Quintenz for the formatting, cover, and website. My amazing family, especially Sid and Jil, who laughed in all the right places and cheered me on at every turn. And Jacob, for always encouraging his nervous mother, and doing the music for the audiobook—coming soon to a device near you.

ABOUT THE AUTHOR

Karen is a lot like her character, Billie. She was an actress, singer, and dancer, before becoming a writer. Sometimes she can't tell where Billie ends and she begins, except Billie is having a bigger life.

You can sign up for the author's newsletter at KarenBerger.net to hear about new releases, videos, and appearances.

If you enjoyed the book, please take a moment to write a review.

www.ingramcontent.com/pod-product-compliance
Lightning Source LLC
Chambersburg PA
CBHW021042130626

46552CB00005B/1973